# Grudges, Goldenrods, and Ghosts

# Also by Tina D.C. Hayes

PETAL PUSHERS MYSTERY SERIES
*Poison, Perennials, and a Poltergeist*
*Secrets, Snapdragons, and a Spirit*

ROCK CANDY ROMANTIC SUSPENSE
*Nefarious*

*No More Tears*

# Grudges, Goldenrods, and Ghosts

Petal Pushers Mystery Series, Book 3

Tina D. C. Hayes

Hazy Moon Ink

ISBN-13: 978-0692583548
ISBN-10: 0692583548

1st Edition

Hazy Moon Ink

# Grudges, Goldenrods, and Ghosts

Petal Pushers Mystery Series, Book 3

Tina D. C. Hayes

Hazy Moon Ink

Copyright © 2015 by Tina D. C. Hayes.

ISBN-13: 978-0692583548
ISBN-10: 0692583548

1st Edition

Hazy Moon Ink

# Prologue

*Only thing that brings me any comfort on days like this is running my fingertips over the pretty clock Darci made out of my broken dish. Like I always said, if this china could cross the Atlantic Ocean in one piece, surely to goodness I can make it through whatever small crisis comes into my life.*

*Well, this situation is a far cry from small, but come hell or high water, I've got to see it through. The secret cain't stay hidden any longer or I never will have any peace. I'm so worried about Darci, though, with Clydell comin' around. That poor girl, bless her heart, she gets into more than enough mischief all by herself.*

*My head is hurtin' somethin' terrible, I guess from worrying so much about all those I hold dear. I cain't bear to lose anybody else.*

*Well, might as well get on with it. I swany, that sure is the yappiest little dog I ever did see. Come on boy, down here. We'll find it this time.*

# Chapter One

*Earth is here so kind, that just tickle her*
*with a hoe and she laughs with a harvest.*
~ Douglas William Jerrold

A gentle breeze swept autumn's first fallen leaves across the grass in a lazy swirl of brown and yellow. Darci brushed her hands off on her jeans and stood back to admire her morning's work. Thanks to a delivery from Simmons' Farm, gourds and winter squash in every shape, size, color, and variety imaginable decorated Petal Pushers' front porch. Hauling pumpkins from the front yard up the steps two at a time provided more of a cardio and resistance workout than she'd bargained for, but she figured it more than made up for her habit of slacking off on exercise.

Cinderella pumpkins looked whimsical beside gooseneck gourds and potted red chrysanthemums grown in the greenhouses out back. Ferns swayed in hanging baskets she'd have to bring inside when the temperature dropped. Traditional orange pumpkins and terra cotta pots of mums lined the steps that lead up to the flower shop. Bales of straw stacked on the far end of the porch were loaded down with patty pan squash and the best prospects for jack-o-lanterns. Paxton was eager to carve some himself, but with Halloween was still five weeks away, he'd have to wait a while yet. She walked back up the front steps, paused long enough to adjust a butternut squash that rolled a few inches from its designated spot, grabbed the newspaper that had bounced off the siding, and then headed inside the shop.

Bells jingled as the door shut behind her.

"How's this look?" Charlotte gestured at the bushels of pumpkins and squash she'd just arranged in the shop's main room. "I've stared at these dang things so long that I'm afraid I overdid it. Looks like the Great Pumpkin exploded in here."

"Looks fine to me." Darci pushed a few small gourds out of the way to make room for the paper and her coffee mug. "The sale we're running on these should thin 'em out pretty soon. If not, we'll just have to turn the extras into enough soup, casseroles, and pies to last us the next ten years."

"Nope, don't think so." Charlotte picked up the empty bushel baskets to take to the work room. "If it comes to that, I'll keep you company, though. Drinking caramel apple martinis while you're up to your elbows in squash casserole and pumpkin guts."

Her muscles ached from lugging all those pumpkins around, so Darci sank into the chair behind the counter for a well-deserved coffee break. An article on the front page of the county paper caught her eye. Burglars had broken into the consignment shop across town, the third such robbery in the area to take place in as many weeks. This was the first she'd heard about it. Why hadn't Max told her about the break-ins, she wondered, but the reason was obvious. Her godfather probably just didn't want her to worry about this crime spree, especially since she'd barely managed to dodge a bullet last year.

Or more to the point, Max wouldn't want her to get any ideas about helping him crack the case. He'd paid her a visit in his capacity as sheriff just a few months earlier, to tell her to quit snooping around Clydell Manor if she didn't want Stetson to press charges. Of course, he'd apologized for not hearing her out on the matter when she dug up a century-old murder victim who proved to be her friend Ellen's long-dead, long-lost great-grandpa. But he'd made it clear that for future reference, she needed to leave any and all detective work up to him.

She turned the page hoping to get that set of memories off her mind, but no such luck. Stetson Clydell grinned like a jackass from the top of page three. He was running for Kentucky state representative in the upcoming election so reporters interviewed the county's most famous politician every chance they got.

"Your face will freeze like that if you're not careful." Charlotte grinned down at her when she came back into the room and caught her glaring at the open newsprint. "Why is your nose turned up like that?"

"Stetson and his endless campaigning." Darci held up his picture and mocked his ridiculous expression, stretching a fake smile from ear to ear. "I will literally throw up if I have to call this moron Congressman Clydell."

"I don't get why he bothers you so much. I mean, he's as phony as you'd expect a politician to be, but he's not nearly as bad as his dad."

"True, we can be thankful old Charlie never had bigger ambitions than the mayor's office." Darci dropped the paper on the desk and tapped Stetson's black and white image. "I honestly don't know why Stetson makes my skin crawl, but he just does. Guess I took an instant dislike to him and can't shake the grudge."

The man had never done anything to offend her, to be fair. He'd hired Wade to renovate his house, and even after their 'misunderstanding' last year, Stetson had been nothing less than cordial whenever they ran into each other. But Darci simply could not stand the man. Some inherent characteristic in Stetson hit a nerve whenever she was anywhere near him, or even when he was only a passing thought.

"Miss Addie doesn't seem to be too fond of the guy either." Charlotte shivered, since the temperature in the room had suddenly dropped by at least fifty degrees. An unexplainable gust of wind

6

rattled the newspaper.

"I remember the door slammed shut for no apparent reason the last time Stetson came to the shop, right after a cold spot like this one about froze the fake smile off his stupid face." The parakeet drew Darci's attention, twittering away like crazy, another sure sign the resident ghost was in the room. She glanced from the bird to the newspaper as she attempted to warm the chill bumps off her arms. "Think I know the perfect place for Stetson's picture.

Darci folded the page into a rectangle that perfectly fit into the bottom of Daisy's cage. The parakeet promptly dropped a doo-doo smack dab in the middle of Stetson's picture. That put a big grin on Darci's face and must have appeased Miss Addie as well, since the room returned to its normal temperature.

"What the heck is that?" Noise from out back drew Darci's attention.

"Beats me," Charlotte said, beside her at the window as they peered out to see what was responsible for all the racket.

They listened closer.

"Sounds like something rattling metal, but I don't see anything." Charlotte's forehead scrunched into a sarcastic frown. "Maybe there's a pack of hobos up the big oak tree, chewing their way through a ginormous can of pork 'n' beans."

"Or an old washing machine trying to break in through the wall." Darci turned her head so that one ear was closer to the window as she strained to hear something familiar. "Hey, listen close. Sounds kind of like a muffled bark. You see Peanut out there anywhere?"

They hurried outside to look for the little scamp. If it was him, it sounded like he'd gotten himself into some sort of trouble.

Peanut lived two doors down with his family, the Spencers. The little Boston terrier had been to the shop a bunch of times, usually on a leash trotting beside his mom, Emily. She didn't allow him out of the house alone, since she was afraid the dog would either get run over or dognapped. But that didn't stop Peanut. For the past few weeks, he'd somehow managed to figure out a way to escape the cushy confines of the Spencer home, for some reason preferring to spend his time yapping it up outside the store. Once he'd scratched at the front door and whined, the next time he'd barked at the kitchen window and spun in circles to get their attention, and after that, he'd paced the back yard between the shop and greenhouses, barking his silly self hoarse.

Why the sweet little black and white pooch had developed an obsessive fascination with Petal Pushers, they had no idea. Neither did the Spencers, about how he got out or why he kept making bee-lines to the flower shop.

Outside, Darci and Charlotte checked the shed and the greenhouses but found neither a band of hobos nor Peanut. They were fixing to check the front yard when they discovered the noise was coming from the cellar, the door of which was jiggling. As they approached it, they heard the Boston bark and whine.

"How the heck did he get down there?" Darci unlocked the old door that lead down to the root cellar underneath the flower shop. "Did you go down there this morning?"

"No. Hoyt took those summer decorations down yesterday like you asked him to, to make room for the fall display we've been working on." Charlotte shook her head. "But I think he'd have noticed if Peanut followed him."

"Unless those ever-blaring earbuds drowned out the sound of the dog yapping." Darci strained to yank the heavy door open. Sure enough, there was Peanut, wagging his stubby little tail at them, a big Boston grin on his snout. "Hey boy, whatcha doing in here?"

Instead of running out into the morning sunshine, the dog trotted into the depths of the dark cellar.

"Peanut, here boy." Darci patted her leg to lure the dog back out, but he was too busy barking to pay her any mind.

"Maybe he chased a squirrel down there, or went back after a chew toy." Charlotte pulled the chain to turn on the light bulb so they could see as they made their way down the stairs behind him. The musty subterranean room with the dirt floor was cast into shadows that seemed to move ominously as the bare bulb swayed back and forth between dust clouded spider webs.

The cellar was originally used to store canned goods and extend the shelf life of apples, potatoes, and onions for the winter, but since Darci had bought the place a year and a half ago, she'd filled it with extra floral supplies and holiday decorations. For some reason, Darci always got a case of the willies when she had to go down there. That's why she usually sent Hoyt. Who knew what kind of poison spiders and, God forbid, lethal snakes might be living down in the spooky dampness?

"Peanut!" Darci yelled. "Stop that!"

But he didn't stop, since he seemed to be having so much fun digging a hole in the corner. His little white paws threw dirt behind him as he worked.

Charlotte scooped him up and couldn't help but laugh at the expression on his little face. "Ah, you can't be mad at the little guy. He looks so sorry." She put her cheek up to the pooch's, who struggled to get down and finish his excavation job. "That he got caught."

Darci reached out and petted the pup on the head. "I'm just glad he didn't hurt himself. Bet Emily is worried sick about this little rascal." To the dog she said, "What the heck were you trying to dig up? A fifty-year-old potato?"

"I bet he was chasing after a mole or something. God, I hope it wasn't a rat! I hate those freakin' things." Charlotte shivered, then kissed Peanut on his wet nose. "Good boy, guarding us from those nasty little shits."

"If I find one piece of rat poop, I'll run in and call the exterminators." Darci glanced around to check for beady eyes and twitching whiskers. She was scared to death of creepy crawly things, and if she let her mind go to wondering what else could be lurking down there, she'd be too freaked out to stand it. "With any luck, it was just a mole. Why don't you take Peanut home, put the Spencers' mind at ease that he didn't get doggie napped, and I'll clean up the mess he made. Damn, I wish you hadn't mentioned rats."

Charlotte headed up the stairs with the wiggling pooch, one hand on the old wooden rail as her sneakers clumped up the stairs. "Want me to make a donut run on the way back?"

"That would be awesome!" Darci was hopelessly addicted to Krispy Kremes, and after unloading and arranging a ton of pumpkins and gourds, she was starving. "Chocolate glazed custards and a lemon filled one would hit the spot. I'll meet you in the kitchen in about fifteen minutes with a fresh pot of coffee."

Other than a few glittery red Valentine streamers strung across the floor, it didn't look like Peanut had made much of a mess other than the hole. She took a trowel from a hook on the wall beside the rakes and knelt down beside the dog's excavation project, careful not to block the light from the single bulb. She was curious to see what he'd been trying to dig up, but no way was she going to poke her fingers around in a dark hole where some icky thing might be waiting to take a bite of her.

The trowel scraped the bottom of the shallow hole, but there wasn't enough light to see anything. Darci took her cell phone from her back pocket and tapped on the flashlight app. Hopefully, Peanut had been looking for a petrified old bone instead of any type of burrowing vermin. With light aimed at the crevice, she poked the trowel around, thrilled when nothing wiggled under it. She removed a few scoops of soil in search of whatever the dog was after.

Nothing.

One last stab in the center of the hole struck something other than hard packed earth. The sound of metal on metal sent a tinny thunk echoing through the cellar.

The long lost license plate, cow bell, or whatever it was in Peanut's mini-pit promised to be about as intriguing as the garbage can she would toss it in. Even so, curiosity got the better of her. No surprise there. Max and Wade both said she was too nosy for her own good. She had to find out what the heck it was and knew she wouldn't have a minute of peace until she did.

A few minutes later, she had widened the hole enough to see that the object was rectangular and did appear to be some type of metal. After inserting the trowel into the dirt and scoring around it, she finally unearthed something.

"What the hell?"

An old cookie tin. Great. Darci had worked up quite an appetite, fueled even more by the promise of those Krispy Kremes Charlotte should be back with any minute. Her stomach growled at the picture of gingersnaps embossed on the side of Peanut's bounty. That she considered biting into an eighty-year-old cookie bordered on pathetic.

The box rattled when she shook it, but it didn't sound like food inside. It sounded much lighter than cookies.

A cloud took shape between the tin she held and the glow from her cell. It took her a moment to realize she was seeing her own breath. Chill bumps rose on her arms and down the back of her neck. The temperature in the cellar stayed cooler than outdoors so she hadn't immediately noticed when the cold spot settled.

"Miss Addie," Darci said in a low whisper. "Did you hide this tin?" The only other reason she could think of for the Ghost Lady to be here now was if she was trying to warn Darci to get out of the cellar.

Not in the mood to take unnecessary chances, Darci quickly refilled the hole with the loose soil and then hurried up the stairs with the tin tucked under her arm.

"Ouch!"

A splinter had pierced her hand as she slid it along the old wooden stair rail on her way out of the cellar.

Back in the shop, Darci placed the dirty tin on her desk behind the counter while she went to wash up.

With the splinter out of her hand and a Band-aid over the place it had been, she put on a fresh pot of coffee. Her stomach growled while she waited for Charlotte to get her butt back with those donuts. Tempted as she was to see what the metal box held, she thought it best to hold off until Charlotte could be with her. Corrosion and dirt had sealed the thing shut, so it would take them a while to pry it open.

Charlotte came in a few minutes later. As they sat down to coffee and donuts, Darci asked how the reunion between Emily Spenser and Peanut had gone.

"She had no idea the little scamp was missing." Charlotte chewed a bite of her raspberry jelly donut faster so she could tell the story. "The doorbell got her out of bed, I'm pretty sure, since she answered the door tying her bathrobe, and it took her a second to realize it was me holding her pooch."

"That's good. At least she wasn't worried sick." Darci bit into chocolate glazed custard filled pastry and nearly moaned in ecstasy. Nothing better than getting her Krispy Kreme fix.

"Here's the weird part," Charlotte said, pausing to wash down the pastry with a sip of java. "Emily said that ever since Peanut started pulling his Houdini act to sneak out of the house a few weeks ago, she's made sure to put him in his crate whenever he had to be out of her sight. That's where he was supposed to be this morning. Her two-year-old was still in her crib, I know because she ran to check on her to make sure she hadn't been kidnapped." She rolled her eyes. "Anyway, the baby couldn't have opened the crate. Emily swears Peanut was snuggled up in it with his favorite teddy bear when she went to bed last night a little before midnight. She was really freaked out."

"Her husband must have let him out before he

left for work."

"Nope, Josh is on night shift this week. Hasn't been home since ten o'clock last night." Raspberry filling spurted down her chin as she took another bite. She grabbed a napkin to dab it off.

"Maybe the crate wasn't latched all the way," Darci reasoned. "He could've pushed it open and headed for the doggie door."

"Darce, this is Emily's dog we're talking about, remember?" Charlotte smirked as she swallowed. "She's so overprotective of Peanut, I'm surprised she lets him go outside to take a crap. Even then she's right beside him with a two-foot leash. She *so* doesn't have a doggie door."

"Well, I'm sure there's some logical reason. There was an article about a few break-ins happening around here, but I seriously doubt any masked gunmen snuck into Emily's house just to steal Peanut for the fun of locking him in our cellar." Something else occurred to Darci. "I wonder how the heck he managed to get down there in the first place. The door is kind of heavy, hard to open, plus the lock was still on it when we opened it this morning, remember?"

"He must've found a crack to squeeze through," Charlotte said. "You see any rats or moles when you cleaned up Peanut's mess?"

"Nope, but I found something way more interesting." Darci told Charlotte about the old tin she'd dug up.

"Wow," Charlotte said through a full mouth. "What do you think is in it?"

"Probably just old junk, maybe a few forgotten

15

seed potatoes." Darci grinned. "You know me, though. My imagination has been running wild with possibilities. Whatever it is had to belong either to Miss Addie or her kids, since they're the only people who ever lived here in this house."

"Well, I can't believe you haven't already ripped the lid off that sucker to see what's inside." Charlotte drained the last of her coffee and put both of their mugs in the sink. "Come on, let's see what you've got."

"Oh crap, I just had a gross thought." Darci's nose turned up, something that rarely happened in the presence of Krispy Kremes. "You don't think they buried a dead pet down in the cellar, do you? I will absolutely freak out if we open up Frisky's tomb."

The lid was stuck pretty tight, corroded from spending no telling how many years buried in the damp root cellar. They ended up spraying the edge of the lid with WD-40 to loosen it up enough so they could use a flat head screwdriver to lever it off. They bent it in a few places, but it wasn't like the old metal box was a valuable antique.

The contents, however, were a priceless find.

## Petal Pushers Plant Profile for Chrysanthemums

### *Chrysanthemum x morifolium*
### Perennial

**Brief description:** Mums are the most popular fall plants, the star of autumn displays in yards across America. Their flowers bloom in white, red, yellow, orange, brown, purple, and pink, and the plants grow from one to three feet tall.

**Trivia:** Mums symbolize fidelity, optimism, joy and long life. If grown indoors, they help purify the air.

**Growing instructions:** They thrive in full sun and need plenty of water. Pinch the foliage back in summer to get bushier plants.

**Uses:** Every yard should have a few of these, ether in pots or growing in borders or flower beds. They're great in fall displays alongside pumpkins and gourds and all things autumnal.

# Chapter Two

*Autumn is the hush before winter.*
~ French Proverb

The atmosphere changed when they took the lid off.

Daisy went into one of her tweeting frenzies, her little feathery head bobbling as she hopped from her perch to the side of the cage. A cold spot sent a chill through the room. Darci honestly didn't know whether all that or the contents they were about to rifle through were the cause of the hair on her arms standing on end around her fresh goose bumps.

The bells on the front door jingled. Miss Addie had a habit of sounding those bells when certain things piqued her attention or she was trying to communicate, so when Darci and Charlotte jerked their heads from the box to the door, they both expected to it to be shut.

Instead, their first customer of the day came in

to take advantage of the sale Petal Pushers was running on chrysanthemums.

Darci put the lid back on the tin as she exchanged glances with Charlotte. The room remained so cold that she was afraid the woman would see her own breath.

When the customer rubbed her hands together and blew on them for warmth, Darci had to say something. "Afraid we're having a little issue with the air conditioner. Let me show you those mums."

A few minutes later, the lady left the still chilly store with three orange mums and a business card. When the door closed behind her, the sign seemed to reposition itself so that it read 'Closed' from the front porch.

Darci flipped it back around. "Sorry about the interruption, Miss Addie, but I'm afraid I can't afford to close up shop just to look through your treasure box."

The parakeet twittered even louder then, which made Darci think the ghost must be waiting near the birdcage behind the desk where the box sat waiting.

"From her reaction, I don't think there's any doubt the box was Miss Addie's, and that she wants us to see what's inside." Charlotte smirked. "So it's probably not a kitty cat corpse."

"You're right." Darci smirked back. "Why would our ghostly friend want us to dig up mummified pets? That would be just ridiculous, now, wouldn't it?"

"Enough with the sarcasm, Darce," Charlotte

said. "Let's pop this sucker back open before she freezes us out."

Darci lifted one corner of the lid but then shut it again. "Think we ought to call Hattie first?"

"No," Charlotte said as if explaining something to a toddler. "She'll want to find out what's in it, which we still don't know yet. She would probably want me to kick your butt if you don't get the lead out before another customer comes in here."

"Fine." Darci took a deep breath before she carefully lifted the lid off the box and placed it on the desk. "Let's see what we've got here."

The contents were mostly paper. She spotted a return address on a stack of letters tied together with a yellow ribbon. They were from Betsy, the last one postmarked in 1941.

"Who are these pictures of?" Charlotte picked up some black and white photographs that had been under the letters. Closer scrutinization made the answer obvious. "The twins! Look Darce!"

Sure enough, the picture showed two beautiful dark haired girls who had to be Betsy's daughters, Ella and Emma. Betsy had been Miss Addie's best friend. They'd learned all about her a few months ago when Betsy's great-grandchildren had made a visit to Webster County.

"That must be Betsy standing beside them in this one." That picture portrayed a middle-aged woman beside a rose bush, her arms around the full-grown identical daughters who stood on either side of her. "Ellen has her eyes and nose, but that smile is all Shane."

21

"Oh, this is so cool!" Charlotte practically devoured the images on the photographs. "What do you think is in those letters?"

"No idea. But what I'd really like to know is how this stuff came to be buried in our cellar?" Darci fidgeted with the ribbon that held the envelopes together.

"What else is in here?" Charlotte dipped her hand back into the box and came out with a yellowed index card. "A recipe for Betsy's hearty harvest soup."

"Yummy, I'll have to try this one out." Darci put the recipe on top of the letters. She thought the metal box was empty, but shook it for good measure. Something inside rattled.

She turned in on its side and ran her fingers around the corners. They'd overlooked one small object.

"Ha! Wonder what this goes to?" Darci held the tiny key up so she and Charlotte could look at it.

"You think Miss Addie kept a diary?"

"I doubt it. She lived alone after Walt died so she wouldn't have needed to lock it, regardless." She turned the little brass key over and set it in her palm. "Hmmm, don't some old clocks have keyholes? For what purpose I have no idea, but don't they?"

"I don't know." A mischievous sparkle lit up Charlotte's eyes. "Ole Addie might have had a chest full of sex toys locked away for those lonely nights. Wouldn't it be a hoot if we found—" Charlotte yelped. She spun around to look behind her.

"What's the matter with you?" Darci had no

idea why her cousin had hollered.

"Okay, sorry, I was just kidding." Charlotte had gone pale as she spoke to thin air. Then she turned to Darci. "She pulled my hair to get me to hush about her, um . . . the things I know a lady like her would certainly not have owned." She cast a wary glance around the room.

Darci doubled over laughing.

Darci and Charlotte wasted a whole lot of time that day scouring the building. Their imaginations had the best of them and they just knew there had to be a lock somewhere in the house that Miss Addie's tiny little key fit into. They took everything out of the kitchen cabinets and used a flashlight to inspect inside every inch of them. Every original closet and the bathroom got the same treatment. All they found were places that needed to be spring cleaned.

Darci didn't want to spend any more time than she had to down in the cellar, especially after the creepy feeling she got right after she found the metal box. She'd never been claustrophobic, but when she'd felt like the walls were closing in on her, a weird and illogical fight or flight compulsion had taken over. She rubbed the Band-Aid on her hand. She didn't even remember gripping the old banister while she walked up the stairs, but apparently she'd clutched it hard enough to embed a splinter so deep she had to use tweezers to dig it out. She'd felt a rush of excitement when she realized the box might hold another connection to her favorite ghost, and reasoned that her adrenaline might be to blame for her anxiety and the injury on her hand.

She sent Charlotte home an hour after her shift was over. Bless her heart, Charlotte was so good to her, always there when she needed help or moral support, or like today, when the nosy streak that ran in their family had them both chomping at the bit to find Miss Addie's locked hiding place that most likely existed only in their imaginations. She was glad her cousin was home now, chasing after baby Cole as he toddled around their house in search of cookies and toy trucks.

On her hands and knees in the store's main room, she was ending her day the same way she'd started it. Moving those damn pumpkins around. They'd moved a table across the room so they could stand on it to look at a curious knothole in the crown molding after Charlotte convinced her it looked like a keyhole. It wasn't, of course. In hindsight, why the heck would it have been? Anyway, now Darci had to pile an assortment of winter squash back on the table and rearrange them as they'd been earlier. She was thinking about how great it would be to soak in a steaming hot bubble bath when she heard someone behind her.

"Hey there, Darci Doodle. How's the world treatin' you today?"

She'd know that voice anywhere, and it put a big goofy smile on her face even before she turned around.

"Evening' Max." Darci stood up and hugged her favorite lawman. "I'm fine, how're you?"

"If I was doin' any better, I wouldn't be able to stand myself."

His uniform wasn't wrinkled or dirty, which led Darci to believe he'd spent most of his day at the office instead of out chasing down dangerous criminals. A low crime rate was one of the many perks to living in a small town.

"Mae wanted me to swing by and give you these." Max plunked a jar of homemade dill pickles on the counter. "She knows they're Paxton's favorite."

"Thank her for me," Darci said. "And yep, he loves his Aunt Mae's kosher dills."

They shot the breeze for a few minutes before Max mentioned the other reason he'd stopped by.

"You hear about those break-ins that have been happening around here lately?" Max picked up a small dipper gourd and tossed it from hand to hand.

"Yep, but I didn't know anything about it until I saw the article in the paper this morning." Darci traced her finger around the jar lid. "Got any leads on who's the mastermind behind it?"

"Not really. They're hitting local businesses, so I thought you might want to beef up security around Petal Pushers, just to be on the safe side." She could tell by his voice that he meant it, but that he didn't want to sound worried about the matter.

"I can't really afford to put in an alarm." Darci

grinned at him. "I could try to get Daisy to bark like a guard dog, if you think that'd help."

"If you just double check to make sure the place is locked up tight before you leave at night, I think that should pretty much take care of it." Max put the gourd down and leaned his elbows beside it on the counter. "And you might ought to lock the door whenever you and Charlotte are here alone at the shop after hours."

Darci felt a wave of panic flitter down her spine. She knew beyond a shadow of a doubt that he wouldn't even bring this up with her unless he thought her flower store might be in the burglar's sites.

"Um, how worried do I need to be about this?" Darci's nervous habit kicked in and she fidgeted with the pickle label. "Should I have Hoyt work the afternoon shift, walk me to my car?"

"No, you don't need to get yourself all worked up over this," Max said. "The break-ins have all been in during the night when nobody was in the buildings."

"Good, that makes me feel better." The last thing she wanted was to be the target of an armed robbery.

"One thing you could do, just as an extra deterrent, would be to put a sticker on your front door that says the store is monitored by a security company. Might make somebody think twice before they try to jimmy the lock."

"That I can do. If you tell me where to get one."

"I'll bring you one tomorrow." Max stood up straight. "One other thing. Don't go tryin' to figure out who the burglars are, because all you'll do is get yourself in trouble. The last thing my poor nerves can handle right now is having to pull your butt out of the fire again."

"Oh, don't be silly," Darci said, punctuating the sentence with a nervous giggle. "You know-"

"I know full well that I remember having a talk with you after that incident when you thought Stetson hid a dead body in his attic." Max wagged his finger at her despite the amused sparkle in his baby blues. "Not to even mention the time I had to serve you with a restraining order."

"Ole Charlie Clydell lied about—"

"I know he can be a peckerwood," Max said, "but you don't need to put yourself in that position. You've been lucky so far with your amateur detective stunts, but I don't want to see you get hurt, or thrown in the slammer for trespassing or God knows what else you might get into."

"Enough with your over reacting," Darci said. Max was totally accurate with everything he'd just said, but she had no intention of putting herself in harm's way, or admitting it. "Don't worry, I'm perfectly happy leaving this case in your capable hands."

"So glad you think I can do my own job, but thanks," Max said, grinning from ear to ear.

"Hey, let me show you what I found this morning." Darci took the old cookie tin from her desk and plopped it down in front of him. She felt like a second grader on show-and-tell day as she filled him in on how they'd found it. She removed the lid and showed him the contents. "Now aren't

27

you glad my mind is preoccupied with this instead of that crime spree?"

"Yep, but I don't doubt your ability to let curiosity get the better of you." Max tapped the tin. "This is interesting, though."

"Any idea what this goes to? Charlotte and I searched every square inch of this place except the attic and that spooky cellar, but we couldn't find anything." Darci swiveled the little key between her fingertips before she held it out to Max. "Could it be a skate key, or fit an old glove box? What do you think?"

"What on earth makes you think Addie Brown took up roller skating in her seventies?" He shook his head and took a closer look at the key. "Any good gossip in those letters?"

"Haven't got to read 'em yet, but I'll probably start on them tonight." Darci ran her fingers over the ribbon that bound the envelopes in the box. "And I do not gossip."

"Yeah, whatever you say, Darce." Max turned the key over in his calloused palm. "You might want to check with the bank. Pretty sure this is an old deposit box key. My dad used to have one that looked a whole lot like this."

After Max left the shop, Darci was so excited about the possibility of the key opening a safety deposit box, she decided to go ahead and give Hattie a call. Miss Addie's granddaughter would surely be tickled to death about what she'd found in the cellar, plus there was no way Darci could go to the bank without first clearing it with Hattie. With any luck, she hoped Hattie could drive up from Clarksville, Tennessee, so they could open it together. She'd have to go to the bank to confirm there was a reason for the trip first, obviously.

It was five minutes until closing. After a quick glance out the window and down the street to convince herself that a horde of customers wasn't fixing to stampede the flower shop, she flipped the sign to 'Closed' and made sure every lock on the property was securely in place. She'd have Hoyt install padlocks on both greenhouses tomorrow. Max hadn't divulged exactly what the burglars had stolen during the break-ins, but she wasn't about to risk letting someone make off with anything she was working so hard to pay for. Feeling safe with the porch light on even before darkness fell, Darci dialed Hattie's number.

"It's so nice to hear your voice, Darci." Hattie was just about one of the sweetest ladies Darci had ever met, polite, genial, and more alert than most folks her age. "How are you?"

"I'm all right, and I hope you are too because I've got one heck of a surprise for you." Darci filled her in on the metal box, the letters and photographs inside, and the key.

"Yes, dear, please," Hattie said, breathless with emotion, "by all means go ahead and read those letters and check out things at the bank. Just promise me you'll let me know what you find out. I doubt Grandma had anything very valuable, but wouldn't it be lovely if she'd put back something with sentimental value?" Hattie often went wistful when speaking of her Grandma Addie, and now nostalgia played heavily in her voice. "I sure would love to hold something of hers in my hands, an old watch or coin she'd held, just anything. That pin she passed on to me is honestly one of my most prized possessions, simply because Grandma loved it so much."

"You might not want to get your hopes up about the deposit box," Darci said. "I'm not even sure the key actually goes to one, but it's the best guess so far. I'd say the real treasure here would be in the letters from Betsy to Miss Addie. Oh, did I mention there was a recipe for Betsy's homemade vegetable soup? Anyway, I can't wait for you to come up to visit so I can give these things to you."

"Oh Darci, I'd hop in the car and make Gene drive me up tonight if I felt up to it." Hattie sighed into the receiver. "But soon, though."

"Sorry you're not feeling well." Darci sincerely meant it. She hated to hear the regret in Hattie's voice, and she thought she detected some worry along with it. "Are you okay? Not trying to be nosy, but I hope it's nothing serious."

"That's sweet, dear." Darci could almost feel Hattie's sweet smile through the phone lines. "I've been a little under the weather here lately, just tired and having some indigestion. Most likely I'm just worn out from all those tomatoes I've been putting up, or it could be a touch of the flu. But don't let me worry you. I'm not even as uncomfortable as Gene, with his sciatica flare ups."

"Well, if you're not back up to par in the next few days, you should see a doctor." Right after the words came out of her mouth, Darci felt like a busybody know-it-all and hoped Hattie didn't think she was overstepping. She would have told her own Grandma Odette the same thing. "You know, just so he can either give you the all clear or prescribe something to perk you right up."

"I'm sure it'll pass before then." Hattie cleared her throat. "But I'd consider it a great big favor if you read through those letters and let me know what's in them, as soon as it's convenient for you. Same with the bank. It'll be nice to know what sort of things Grandma and Betsy talked about."

And that was exactly what Darci intended to do that night as soon as she got home, cooked dinner, and cleared away the last dirty dish. Hattie sounded like she'd be plum disappointed if she didn't hear from her real soon, so she hoped to find a few interesting details to pass along to her.

## Betsy's Hearty Harvest Soup

### Ingredients:
1 large onion, chopped
2 garlic cloves, minced
1 medium carrot, chopped
2 cups spinach or your favorite greens, coarsely chopped
4 TBSP butter or margarine
1 large potato, whole and unpeeled
2 cups cooked pinto beans, drained
4 cups vegetable stock
3 cups water
1 can pumpkin puree
3/4 cup corn, fresh off the cob or frozen
1 TBSP dried thyme
1 TBSP dried oregano
2 or 3 dashes of ground red pepper, to taste
1 to 1-1/2 TBSP salt, to taste
 Pepper to taste
Green onions, for garnish

### Directions:
Melt the butter or margarine over medium-high heat in a Dutch oven. Add onion and carrot, then cook until the onions are transparent. Add the spinach and garlic, cook about a minute or so to start wilting the greens, then add the vegetable

stock, water, pumpkin, whole potato, beans, corn, the spices, and 1 tablespoon of the salt. Cook until the potato is done, about half an hour or so, and then take it out of the pan. When the potato cools just enough to handle, peel it and mash the potato good with a fork, and then add it back to the soup for a nice creamy texture. Taste it and add more salt and pepper if needed.

Pour the soup into serving bowls, sprinkle with chopped green onion, and serve with toasted chunks of bread.

# Chapter Three

*And the Autumn clutches the forests green*
*In a hasty and eager clasp;*
*But the leaves are true to the Summer they love,*
*And they wither and fade in his grasp.*
~ J.J. Britton

Exhausted from hauling pumpkins around the shop all day, Darci went to bed early that evening. Wade and Paxton were watching *The Minions* on DVD downstairs in the living room, but since she couldn't get her mind off the tin she found in the cellar that morning, she'd headed upstairs with the last piece of chocolate pie and the stack of old letters. She wouldn't have had the strength to walk up the steps if she'd conked out on the couch, and since she hadn't stuck to her plans for getting into shape, she didn't delude herself into thinking Wade could carry her without a forklift. She sighed, then dug into her pie and the first letter.

The correspondence between Betsy and Miss Addie wasn't particularly exciting, other than the fact that Darci felt a connection to both women. Her eyes blurred from exhaustion about halfway through the third letter. She set it on her nightstand with the others, slid her empty plate to the side so as not to smudge the yellowed stationery with chocolate, and she went out like an old light bulb.

The next morning didn't find her well-rested despite her having hit the hay before ten o'clock. Bad dreams snatched her awake at least three times, and their images ran through her mind as she got ready for work. Not scary enough to qualify as nightmares, her dreams were more unpleasant and eerie than anything, probably due to the box she'd found buried in the cellar along with the talk she'd had with Max about the local burglaries.

She'd dreamt she had to go to the cellar to get something. Another splinter from the old railing got caught on her palm when she was halfway down the stairs. The room began to spin, and she felt like she was on a carnival ride gone out of control. She made her way to the bottom and found Peanut, a buttery yellow bow tied around his neck, barking at a pile of newspapers. Broken jars littered the ground, their sticky red contents smeared across the dirt floor. Afraid the dog would cut his feet on the glass shards, she picked up the Boston terrier and ran to the door.

It would not open. As she banged her fist against it, a loud and disturbing noise echoed up the stairs behind her, raising the hair on the back of her neck even after she woke up in a cold sweat.

As she made cinnamon toast for breakfast, she blamed her lack of sleep for her splitting headache. She took two Tylenol and almost gagged on the orange juice she washed them down with.

At the shop that morning, Darci set the bundle of letters on her desk beside the metal box and headed for the kitchen to put on a pot of coffee. She would need to keep her caffeine level pretty high or else her lack of sleep would make her groggy and grumpy the rest of the day, which wasn't the best way to endear herself to new customers.

The scent of brewing coffee wafted behind her as she took a seat at the desk. Reading more of the letters would have to wait until later, so she tucked the stack into the cookie tin and took out the tiny key. Her fingertips played over the key's surface as she swiveled around in the chair, her gaze falling on the mosaic clock on the wall as she planned out her schedule. Prepping bridal flowers would keep her busy most of the day, and she needed to walk over to the bank that afternoon to talk to Mel Harper. He should be able to tell her whether or not the key went to a safety deposit box, and if so, if it would open one in their vault. Of course, the chances of their keeping an abandoned safety deposit box over the decades were pretty slim, and she figured the bank would have upgraded to a newer design at least once since 1941.

"What the—" Darci stared at her empty hand. Where had the key gone? She didn't think she was stupid enough to lose something while sitting still, but she had no recollection of putting it down. She dropped to her hands and knees and crawled around on the floor to look for it. She would never forgive herself if she had to tell Hattie she'd lost Miss Addie's key before they even found out for sure what it opened.

"Morning, Boss Lady." She bumped her head on the bottom of the counter when Hoyt came in the back door. "What are you doing under there?"

"Trying to find something I dropped." Darci ran her hand along the baseboards beneath the counter. "That little key I showed you yesterday."

Hoyt squatted down to help her search until the phone rang. He answered it, and she heard him repeat Jed Hamilton's order of a birthday bouquet for his wife for confirmation before he ended the call. He ripped a sheet off the order pad, and then Darci saw his shoes approach as she crawled around under the marble top table in front of the porthole window.

"Found it." Hoyt bent down to show her the key on his open palm.

"Great, thanks." Darci stood and took it from him. "Where was it."

"On the desk beside the phone." Hoyt adjusted his earbuds before he took the order he'd jotted down to the workroom so Charlotte could get started on it when she came in.

How in the hell had she somehow managed to drop it on the desk? She'd been a few yards away from it the last she remembered holding the key.

"Be right back to feed you, Daisy," Darci said to the parakeet as she walked past her cage to put the key back in the tin for safekeeping. "Right after I guzzle some coffee. Either I'm more tired than I thought or I'm losing my mind."

"Mornin' Darce." Charlotte nearly always brightened the place up when she came in.

"Morning." Darci grinned over her coffee cup. "How's Cole doing? Poor little guy, cutting those back teeth."

"I think he's over the worst of it, thank goodness." Charlotte took a seat next to Darci's, as was her habit. They liked to talk for a few minutes before she dove into her work day. "Orajel and those frozen teether toys he gnaws on do the trick."

"That's good. I hate to see him fussy and achy." Darci loved her baby cousin and jumped at every opportunity to babysit. Charlotte brought him to work whenever her sitter had the day off, so they kept an extra playpen set up upstairs. Whenever Cole was there, Darci spent more time playing with the toddler than hawking flowers.

"He was gurgling through a mouthful of ap-

39

plesauce when I left. Ashley probably has it in her hair, but she never seems to mind." Charlotte scrolled through the latest social media notifications on her cell before she checked their calendar. "We got anything major going on today?"

"Hoyt took an order for a bouquet this morning." Darci glanced at the to-do list she kept on her desk. "Other than that, we just have to prep for the Brenner-Vincent wedding this weekend and finish up those centerpieces for the Chamber of Commerce banquet."

"I hope Hoyt jotted down all the particulars." Charlotte shook her head. "Couple weeks ago, he left me a slip of paper that said 'flowers for Eddy's grandma.' I was like, what the hell Hoyt! How was I supposed to know whether that meant a potted plant or a funeral spry, plus I know about five Eddys."

Darci grinned. "I have no idea what he wrote down, but he left the order in the workroom. I'll be able to tell by the cussin' or the lack thereof whether it's up to your standards."

Betsy's hearty harvest soup with toasty warm corn muffins was on the menu for their lunch break a few hours later. After finding the recipe card yesterday, Darci had bought the ingredients on her way home and whipped up a batch. It was so good! Darci added fresh chopped green onions to the bowls and sat down as Charlotte entered the room and sat across from her.

"What did you find out at the bank?" Charlotte spooned soup into her mouth and gave the thumbs up.

"Haven't been yet," Darci said. "I'll try to go this afternoon, if I get a chance."

"I looked through the stuff in the box after I waited on the lady who bought a succulent pot. The key wasn't in there, so I assumed you'd already checked with Mel about it," Charlotte said.

"What?" Darci nearly choked. She wiped up the muffin crumbs that spurted out of her mouth, shaking her head as she swallowed. "That key should be in the bottom of the tin. You sure it's not there?"

"I didn't see it."

Darci hurried up front to have a look. She put the bundle of letters on her desk blotter, the recipe card beside it, and then carefully set the photos on top of that. No key. She turned the cookie tin upside down and banged the bottom of it, but nothing fell out.

"Where's the last place you remember having it?" Charlotte followed her up front still nibbling on a corn muffin.

"I misplaced it this morning, but Hoyt found it, and then I know I put it here in the box underneath the letters." Darci pointed inside the empty tin. "I don't understand where the dang thing could be, unless we have a pack rat running loose through the store.

"Come on back to the kitchen and finish eating," Charlotte said, putting her arm around her shoulder after she took the box from her hands and set it down. "You'll feel better on a full stomach. I'll help you look for it then."

"Maybe I've lost what little mind I had left,"

41

Darci said as she retook her seat and picked up her spoon. "I *know* I put it back in there."

"Try not to think about it for a few minutes or you're gonna give yourself a nasty case of heartburn." Charlotte added a few dashes of pepper to her bowl.

"Didn't get much sleep last night. You think I could've conked out, sleep walked the key to some weird hiding place, and then woke up without any idea of what I'd just done? Maybe?"

"Um, no." Charlotte raised an eyebrow. "I think you're just freaking out a little."

After they finished lunch, they went back up front, Darci on her hands and knees crawling around for the second time that day and Charlotte on the other side of the counter, looking under each and every gourd before she moved on to the floor on that side.

"You fidget so much, you probably picked it up without thinking about it. Especially with you being dog tired."

"That's a distinct possibility, but I hope not. I don't usually fiddle around with anything important." Darci dumped out the trash can and began sorting through the contents.

"Well, that's a lot more likely than you sleep walking off with it," Charlotte said. "Unless you suddenly developed amnesia and narcolepsy."

They slowly made their way around the room without any luck. Darci went back to check the notepad by the phone where Hoyt had found it earlier, just in case Miss Addie was playing some kind of game with it.

Nada.

Daisy's tweeting drew their attention. The little parakeet hopped around her cage as if something had startled her. The bird finally settled on a perch in the top corner, then turned her little feathered head to peer at Darci as if waiting for her to do something.

"What's the matter, girl?" Darci went to the cage and peeped inside. Nothing seemed to be out of place. Then she thought to check the bird's water dish to make sure a bug hadn't landed in it. A horsefly drowned in it recently and Daisy had refused to go near it until she had fresh water.

Darci drew in a sharp, audible breath.

"What's the matter? Daisy's not sick, is she?" Charlotte hurried over to make sure the shop mascot was alright.

Darci shook her head, her index finger pointed toward the water dish in the birdcage.

"That is weird," Charlotte said after taking a glance. "Any idea how it got there?"

"No. You know how careful I am about feeding Daisy. I wash her dishes every morning. No way in hell I plopped that key into her dish. It might have germs on it, as old as it is." Darci quickly removed the water dish from the cage, even though the bird wasn't going anywhere near it. "If Hoyt is messing with me, I swear I'll kick his butt. Here, hold this."

She gave Charlotte the wet key before stomping off to the kitchen to clean out Daisy's dish. "Do *not* put that thing down until I get back."

After she'd washed it out with dish soap and sterilized it with steaming water from the tea kettle, Darci put the clean bowl of fresh water back in the cage.

"You still have it?" Darci held out her palm and Charlotte handed her the key.

Darci reached behind her neck to unfasten her necklace, a slim gold chain with a flower charm. "Okay, you're my witness." She threaded the key onto the chain before she fastened it securely back around her neck. "This isn't coming off until I can personally give it to Hattie."

"Mel Harper will love that." Charlotte flashed her wicked grin.

"Why?" Darci had no idea what she was getting at.

"Because he'll have great cleavage view when you show it to him."

## Petal Pushers Plant Profile for Pumpkins

***Cucurbita pepo***
**Annual vegetable**

Pumpkins are a variety of winter squash, which share the same genus species. In this profile, I'm talking about the classic round orange ones we carve into jack-o-lanterns at Halloween and turn into pies at Thanksgiving.

**Trivia:** Before Irish immigrants came to America, they carved jack-o-lanterns out of turnips and potatoes, to ward off evil spirits. Pumpkins worked much better, and a new tradition was born. Otherwise, you'd be out shopping for Halloween turnips.

**Growing instructions:** Plant seeds one inch deep, four or five seeds per hill. They should come up in about five to ten days.

**Uses:** Pumpkins are the main focus in most fall displays, inside and outdoors. Other than jack-o-lanterns and pies, you can use pumpkins as doorstops, hollowed out ones can be containers to serve dip or soup out of, and small ones can be used as place cards. Pumpkin flowers are edible. Don't you dare throw away those pumpkins seeds, since you can toss them with spices and roast them up for a delicious snack. You can find about a million other ideas for what to do with pumpkins on Pinterest.

# Chapter Four

*Every leaf speaks bliss to me,*
*Fluttering from the autumn tree.*
~ Emily Brontë

Turned out the bank would have to wait a couple of days. Not long after they found the key in Daisy's cage, Darci got an urgent call for funeral flowers. The deceased had been dead a few days, so that wasn't the emergency.

The lady who called, Gloria Newman, had gotten miffed at the first florist she'd hired to do the job. She'd ordered a baby blue arrangement and spray for her uncle's casket. Instead, they delivered flowers in some funky purple shade, and then had the gall to argue with her right there in front of poor Uncle Joe's coffin. Gloria said she told them to send that crap back to whatever circus they stole it from and canceled the rest of her order, thus the need for emergency flowers. And the funeral service was scheduled for nine o'clock the next morning.

"Oh lord," Charlotte said when Darci hung up the phone. "What if that woman gives us three kinds of hell after we make the delivery? You think she might try to pull a scam or something and not pay us, or do you think she's just super picky?"

"We shall see." Darci clicked some keys on the computer to bring up Petal Pushers' email. "She's fixing to send pictures of the quote 'crappy ass weed garland' the other florist sent."

"What if it turns out she's color blind? Purple and light blue aren't all that far apart on the color spectrum," Charlotte pointed out.

"She said the flowers were dyed the color of a neon grape popsicle." Darci was a bit skeptical herself.

Gloria Newman's email popped up. Darci clicked on it and opened the two attached pictures.

"Oh. My. God." Darci's mouth dropped open and Charlotte's eyes threatened to pop out of their sockets. "That really is one hot mess."

"Damn straight. Looks like the Grape Ape took a piss all over everything," said Charlotte. "If she didn't filter in that purple tint, I agree with her. I'd have told the florist to go f—"

"Not tampered with," Darci interrupted. "Look, right there."

Charlotte leaned closer to the screen.

"The kid's candy? Okay, I can run out to the store and pick up something for your sweet tooth, but what's that have to do with this?"

"No, smart aleck. You can't argue with the taste of the rainbow, or the colors either." Darci tapped the screen again. "The picture shows that little girl's Skittles package true to color. Compare that to this floral train wreck, there's no doubt they botched the job."

"So," Charlotte poked the screen on her cell phone. "How late should I ask Ashley to babysit?"

They ordered a pizza for supper at the shop. In light of the burglaries, Hoyt stayed to help them until ten. Darci cringed thinking about how much she was going to have to pay out in overtime, but Charlotte and Hoyt deserved it, and both did an excellent job. She and Charlotte called it a night at the witching hour. Not only did they have to scramble to make a memorial wreath and casket spray to order—in just the right shade of baby blue so as not to further piss off the Newmans—but when Gloria had it out with the florist she'd fired, her friends and relatives had canceled their orders as well. Uncle Joe must have been a pretty nice guy because the phone at Petal Pushers had blown up.

The following day was pretty hectic as well. Darci and both of her employees came in early to put on the finishing touches and load the delivery van. Gloria was very pleased with their efforts and thanked Darci through teary eyes. By the time she and Hoyt made the drive back to the shop, Charlotte looked frazzled.

"Heck, I forgot the fall sale started today." Darci was thrilled to see so much of their fall display had been sold, but could tell Charlotte was worn out from waiting on customers all morning. "But today is going to look good on paper when I do the books."

She called Hattie to let her know about the delay. Shocked by how frail her elderly friend sounded, Darci was worried sick and made her promise to see a doctor the following day. Hattie promised, and told her she didn't have to be in a hurry about the key and such. "We didn't even know that stuff existed last week. It'll keep until you find the time, one that's convenient for you, dear."

After she hung up, Darci emailed Ellen. She wanted to let her know about the tin she'd found and promised to send copies of the pictures of Betsy and the twins.

Darci finally managed to get away from Petal Pushers during banker's hours a few days later. They had tied up all the details for the big wedding, so with Charlotte in charge of things at the shop and Hoyt running the last deliveries of the day, Darci walked down the sidewalk toward the center of town. The afternoon sun cast elongated shadows that made her dark alter ego appear much taller and thinner than her Krispie Kreme habit allowed her real body to achieve.

She fidgeted with the key as she walked, sliding it back and forth on her necklace. The thing seemed to have a mind of its own and she was still scared to death of losing it. There was no explanation for how it magically ended up in the bird's water bowl, since it wasn't likely that a dropped object could fall *up* to the cage that sat at eye level, fit between the bars, and splash land in the dish.

Good thing the dainty gold chain had been a gift rather than the cheaper type she would have bought herself. She had kept it on, even in the bathtub, for fear of the key walking off again.

Miss Addie must have something to do with the key playing hide and seek, but it didn't make any sense. Ever since Darci had dug up the cookie tin, she'd noticed something creepy at the shop. A sensation of being watched, a feeling that she wasn't alone. Miss Addie gave her goosebumps with her cold spots while her presence always felt friendly, familiar, and loving.

Now Darci was getting the willies. What if the eerie feeling in the shop was due to burglars staking out the store? Darci couldn't afford a break-in. She'd worked her butt off to open Petal Pushers a year and a half ago, and was even nearing the half-way point of paying off the extra greenhouse she'd had to cough up money for when she'd replaced the one squashed and charred under a tree limb during a storm a few months ago.

Fallen leaves blew over the sidewalk and skittered through the grass. Darci thought this time of year was especially beautiful, with a rainbow of autumn leaves still clinging to the tree branches. Goldenrods bloomed across the Kentucky countryside. The temperature still climbed to warm most days, but the afternoons brought a comfortable coolness that was welcome after the sweltering days of summer. The air just seemed to smell better, and was there anything better than roasting marshmallows under a full moon? That's what she had planned for the weekend, since Paxton invited Jake over to camp out in the backyard.

At the bank, Darci took a seat in Mel Harper's office and chatted with the teller, Suzanne Fleming, while she waited for him. When Mel entered the room, they shook hands before Darci explained what she was there to find out.

"Do you have the key with you? I'd be happy to take a look at it." The banker waited while Darci took the key from her necklace and carefully, very carefully, laid it in his palm. She realized he probably thought she was a nut for wearing it like a charm, but she had no intention of letting it get lost again.

"Hmmm." Mel examined the small key, turned it over and used a magnifying glass to look for something on the back. "Okay," he said, "this doesn't fit any of the safety deposit boxes we have now, but I think it does go to the ones original to the bank. They were replaced in the sixties, and then again during our last remodel about ten years ago."

Darci's heart sank into her socks.

"I was afraid of that." Darci fidgeted with the chair arm. "We knew there wasn't much chance of her belongings still being here after all these years, but it was worth a shot. At least now we know that's what the key actually went to."

"Well, you'll be happily surprised to find out the unclaimed boxes are in storage, intact and unopened." He plunked the key down on his blotter. Darci's eyes kept shifting from it to the bankers face until he finally slid it across the desk to her so she could return it to the safekeeping of her necklace.

"Really? Hattie, that's Miss Addie Brown's granddaughter," Darci explained, "is going to be thrilled to hear that." She stood, eager to see what was inside. "Let's go take a peek."

"Sorry, but that'll have to wait a while."

"Oh?" Darci retook her seat, her hand on the key that hung from her neck to make sure it was still there.

"It's not here, at the bank. There's quite a few of them," Mel said. "They're stored in a safe place, but off site, out of town."

Darci didn't ask where because she figured the location must be a secret if they didn't volunteer the information. She just nodded.

"Tell you what," he said. "I think I can get it for you and your friend Hattie in a few weeks. There's a small number engraved on the edge of those keys, so I can jot it down if you let me see it one more time. Then I'll fill out the paperwork and have it sent over here."

"Sure, here you go." Darci took off her neck-

53

lace and set it on his desk, watching closely as he once again took the magnifying glass to it and made a notation on his notepad before sliding it back to her.

"I'll give you a call when it gets here."

"Donovan!" Darci yelled, pushing past some of the uniformed officers she knew through Max. "Donovan, are you okay?"

She spotted her friend sitting at one of the shampoo stations, his face flushed, wringing his hands.

When he saw her approach, he jumped up and gave her a big bear hug. "Oh Darci, thanks for coming. How did you know?"

"Minerva Clayton came in Petal Pushers this morning and told me all about the break in." Minerva was Deputy Smith's mother and knew Darci and Donovan were buddies. Her son would only give her so much information before he got called away early that morning, so she had mistakenly thought Darci could fill her in on the details of the latest burglary, this one at the Hair Dare Your 'Do Salon. "All she knew about it anyway, which was practically nothing. I asked Charlotte to take over the shop and high-tailed it over here to see how you are." Darci pulled back from his hug to look for clues as to exactly how her friend was holding up.

"No one was here when they broke in, which was a blessing since nobody got hurt." Donovan fanned himself with a hair magazine and took a deep breath to center himself. "I hope to high heaven that my insurance covers cat burglars."

"How bad is it?"

"They emptied the register." Donovan shook his head. "I was supposed to deposit yesterday's till this morning, since I hurried home yesterday instead of taking the time to do it then. We were swamped, I'd been on my feet all day, and all I wanted to do was go home and crack open a nice bottle of pinot noir while I waited for the pizza delivery guy. Was that wrong?"

"Of course not, you work so hard." Darci patted his hand.

"Apparently it was. The robbers broke in during the night, made off with everything we made yesterday. At least Sally took her tip jar with her, or that would've been lost too. Mrs. Clydell was in her chair yesterday, and everybody knows what a big tipper she is. To show off, but still, we appreciate it."

"Was cash the only thing they took?" Darci asked.

"Oh heavens no. That would've been too nice of them." Donovan pulled her over to seats beside the shampoo stations and they both sat down. "They took all the high-end curling wands we had in stock. The good ceramic ones, not the old ones with the clips. Antoine's clippers are gone too. You know he paid way too much for those, but he likes to be flashy. All gone, and he's going to just die when I tell him they're missing."

"I'm so sorry they hit your salon," Darci said.

"Is there anything I can do?"

"No, sweetie, I'm just glad you're here," Donovan said. "Unless you can help me find the S.O.B.s responsible for this, so I can kick their asses and get my stuff back."

Darci sensed he wasn't completely joking. Donovan had helped her snoop around Clydell Manor a few months back and tried to cover up her blunder when she'd thought an old bowling ball was Stetson's dead great-uncle's severed head. They had become close friends over the past year and a half, and his significant other, Bradley, an up-and-coming architect, had paired up with Wade for a few construction jobs, including remodeling Clydell Manor. She felt just awful looking at the state of his hair salon, the front glass busted out, things broken and turned inside out as the robbers hunted for valuables.

"Y'all just leave the crime fighting to me and the boys." Max had overheard Donovan's last comment. Darci hadn't known he was standing right behind her, but at least he hadn't had a good view of her face. She knew her eyes were dancing at the thought of helping her friend get his stuff back.

"Of course we will, Max." Darci tried as hard as she could to look innocent, to keep any hint of mischief out of her voice. "Let us know if there's anything we can do to hurry the investigation along. We'd be happy to help out."

Donovan nodded his enthusiastic agreement but had the good sense not to comment on it.

The expression on Max's face let her know

she'd failed miserably.

# Petal Pushers Plant Profile for Goldenrod

## *Solidago canadensis*
## Perennial

**Brief description:** This herbaceous perennial is a member the Aster family, with a number of different species. Goldenrod grows three to four feet tall, topped with vivid yellow flower spikes in the fall that attract butterflies and bees.

**Trivia:** Goldenrods are the Kentucky state flower. Some people consider them to be signs of good luck. Beyond popular belief, goldenrod doesn't aggravate allergies, since its pollen isn't airborne.

**Growing instructions:** Most people in North America classify this pretty yellow wildflower as a weed. Europeans use them as garden plants, so you might want to see if there's a spot for them in your landscape. Keep an eye on them if you do, since they are very invasive. They thrive in full or partial sun and can be found growing in fields, the forest, and on the side of the road.

**Herbal Uses:** Goldenrod is known for its diuretic, antioxidant, and astringent qualities. Particularly useful for urinary tract disorders, and it can eliminate kidney stones and reduce inflammation.

# Chapter Five

*I cannot endure to waste anything so precious as
autumnal sunshine by staying in the house.
So I have spent almost all the daylight hours
in the open air.*
~ Nathaniel Hawthorne

Darci and Wade settled into bed around midnight. With Paxton and Jake tucked into the tent out back, she left their bedroom window cracked so they could hear the boys if they got loud or hollered for help during the night. The backyard was fenced in, the gate padlocked since she'd found out about the local burglaries, so they were safe from everything except their imaginations. Ten-year-old boys had hellacious imaginations.

Earlier that evening, the boys caught lightning bugs before they gathered around the chiminea on the patio to roast hot dogs. The s'mores were Darci's favorite part. The gooey charred marshmallows sandwiched between Hershey's chocolate and graham crackers rivaled even her beloved Krispy Kremes. She'd sent Wade back out to double and triple check that the fire was completely out, and that neither of the boys had matches. They were good kids, but heaven only knew what sort of ideas lurked in their heads.

They clicked the television on to watch some late night news before they fell asleep. Well, before Darci took a nap, since she knew she'd be up to check on the boys a few times before the sun came up.

Instead of a commentary on the country's latest criminal activity, tonight's news focused on footage from a disaster in the Carolinas. A category five hurricane. Having spent the evening outside with the boys, this was the first either of them had heard of it. Wade had a cousin in South Carolina.

"This is awful!" Darci couldn't believe the destruction in Hurricane Hannibal's path. The newscaster had just said that this was the worst natural disaster to hit the United States since Katrina devastated New Orleans in 2005. "Look at that roof that's barely sticking out of the water."

Wade was already on the phone to his relatives, to make sure his cousin Phil was alright. Luckily, they lived in the central part of the state. Phil and his family were safe in their living room, waiting out the storm, far enough from the coast to escape flood damage.

They watched the heart-wrenching footage until Darci fell asleep curled up beside Wade.

Darci bent down to tie her Nikes. Why her new shoes came with laces long enough to use for jump ropes, she had no idea. She gave up and went with the double knot bunny ear technique she hadn't used since Paxton was four and tripped over his feet all the time.

She hoped walking to the shop would help her burn off all those extra donuts she'd been scarfing down. Between worrying about the burglars that were still on the loose and playing peek-a-boo with the key, no wonder her nerves were a frazzled mess. Donuts were her drug of choice against anxiety and her pusher was Krispy Creme.

After she had opened the shop, she made a cup of coffee, no cream and only a scant sprinkle of sugar, so as not to drink up all the calories she'd burned off on her morning walk. Making handouts for the gardening class she taught was the first thing on her to-do list, so she opened Word and got busy. By the time Charlotte came in, she'd already finished the one on rosehips and started one on frugal houseplants for the following lesson.

"Guess what I got in the mail yesterday?" Darci rolled her eyes and pursed her lips.

"Sour lemons?"

"Those I could have made cocktails with," Darci said. "Wade and I have been cordially invited to a shindig at Clydell Manor to help Stetson celebrate the upcoming election he's pretty sure he's going to win, the pompous ass. Woo hoo, lucky me."

"Looks like Miss Addie doesn't approve either." Charlotte rubbed her arms to indicate the cold spot that settled over them when the Clydell name had come up.

"I sure as heck don't want to go, but Wade said we have to since he has a business relationship with Stetson." Darci smirked. "No way in hell will I vote for him. Not even if his only opponent was a purple pig in a little top hat. Our delivery van would be decorated with purple bacon bumper stickers."

"I'm kind of surprised he's letting Wade bring a plus one. Guess he's not holding it against you that you blackmailed him into picking up the tab for Betsy and Ellis' new burial plots." Charlotte had a valid point.

"It wasn't blackmail." Darci pulled a brown leaf off a miniature rose and twirled it in her fingers, careful of the Lilliputian thorn. "Well, not exactly.""

"Should be a fun party, if you ignore Stetson." Charlotte's eyes lit up and she laughed. "I bet his wife will be just thrilled to see you. Probably greet you at the door with fake European cheek kisses and a cold shoulder."

"Thanks for reminding me." Phoebe Clydell had caught her and Donovan snooping around her home a few months ago. Apparently, it had pissed her off when Darci accused her of keeping her husband's dead ancestor's corpse in their attic. "At least Donovan and Bradley are going. If nothing else, me and Donovan can stand in the center of the room, under Phoebe's watchful eye, and aggravate her by acting like we're up to something. You know she's gonna have the help watch us like hawks, to make sure we don't go back up to the attic or scope out her Prada collection."

"Just relax and enjoy yourself. I sure would. Phoebe Clydell and a few of her snooty friends aside, there should be plenty of interesting people to schmooze with." Charlotte had a point. "Bet the food will be off the charts delicious."

"Hadn't thought of that," Darci said, her mouth watering at the possibility. "Donovan called as soon as he opened his invitation. We're going shopping this Sunday to pick out our outfits. He insists I go by his salon the day of the party to get my hair and makeup done, since the local news and photogs are going to cover the event. We want to look our awesome best, snap a few pictures to put on our websites. You know, to make it look like we hobnob with the rich and famous." Her cheeks burned with embarrassment over that last statement. It didn't help when Charlotte smirked at her, her wrist twisting in a mock royal wave. "Hey, I still don't want to go, but maybe we can use this to our advantage, get a little free publicity for Petal Pushers and the salon."

"Don't forget to take those yellow mums to Mae," Darci reminded Hoyt as he headed toward the door, his arms loaded down with afternoon deliveries. "Promised her I'd get 'em to her before the sun goes down."

"No prob, Boss Lady."

Hoyt tried to hide his grin but she saw it before he disappeared through the doorway.

"Really, you just have to keep calling me that?" She really didn't mind as much as she let on, but if he had to use a nickname, she would definitely prefer something else that didn't make her sound so bossy.

Darci turned her attention back to the design she was sketching. Vera Thompkins from Golden Days Retirement Home asked her to come up with ideas for the gazebo she wanted to put in that coming spring. Vera wanted something snazzy, inviting, comfortable, wheelchair accessible, a beautiful structure the board of directors couldn't possibly say no to when she asked them to work it into the budget. Wade could build it, wouldn't charge much more than the cost of the material, and his crew could assemble the whole thing in two days' time.

Darci imagined the residents sitting in the gazebo drinking lemonade on summer afternoons, probably listening to Bernice dish the latest gossip. Mabel could read her magazines there while she enjoyed the scent of the flowers growing around it. Even old Charlie could sneak out there with his buddies for afternoon poker games, away from the prying eyes of the orderlies who weren't supposed to let them gamble for real money anymore.

She paused to swat at her neck. Must be one of the pesky flies that swarmed in whenever the door was open for a few seconds. Falling temperatures should take care of that problem pretty soon.

Darci's pink coloring pencil added a few clusters of vinca blooms to offset the yellow Stella d'Orzo day lilies and red impatiens she'd drawn around the perimeter of the gazebo, the design of which she'd copied from Wade's sketches. She made sure to include some of the residents' favorite flowers, Confederate jasmine, tiger lilies, and a couple pink rose bushes. Two separate varieties of clematis would vine up the sides and mingle on the roof when full grown, into an artful profusion of purple and white blooms. Now she just needed to add a taller stalky plant toward the back on either side to round out the landscape design.

"Ouch!"

Darci's hand flew to her throat.

"Stop it!"

She sprung out of her seat and turned around. She saw no one.

"Hoyt, you're playing too rough. That's not funny," Darci shouted. "Quit hiding!"

Toots from the delivery van's horn sounded. Through the window, she saw Hoyt pulling out of the driveway, waving at a passing car.

He was the only other person there.

Someone had jerked the chain around her neck and pulled on it. She walked to a mirror that hung on the showroom wall to take a closer look. Sure enough, a raw line encircled her throat. The necklace had been yanked with enough force to leave an impression of the top of the key in her tender skin.

How was this possible?

Something was very, very wrong here.

At that moment, a silver tray that had been sitting on one of the display tables crashed to the floor. At least the crystal candle holders were still in their place, in one piece. The parakeet went into a frenzy and the temperature dropped at least thirty degrees. The air in the room grew dense.

Another quick, violent tug on the necklace made Darci jump.

The cold spot grew so cold that a cloud of her own breath took shape in front of her face.

Daisy's song changed. Usually when Miss Addie made her presence known, the bird would jump on the side of the cage and tweet a happy song as if she expected someone to reach in and take her out. Now, the parakeet had changed her tune from the usual to squawks and shrill whistles. She sat on the swing in the middle of her cage, clearly agitated.

"Miss Addie, what's going on?"

An eerie breeze moved through the room.

Fear gripped Darci's heart. Could ghosts suddenly turn on people like a mad dog infected with rabies? Darci watched enough Sunday afternoon ghost hunting documentaries to find that idea highly unlikely, since she'd never seen an episode where a spirit suddenly went rogue schizophrenic. As a matter of fact, when the homeowners thought they had a moody ghost, there usually turned out to be multiple entities.

More than one!

"Oh hell no!" Darci did not understand what was going on. It made absolutely no sense, since the only person to ever die in the house was Miss Addie Brown, a well-loved woman with a sweet soul, even in the afterlife. Never before had she or Charlotte experienced this malevolent spirit responsible for the abrasion on Darci's neck. "Miss Addie, are we alone?"

A crash sounded behind the counter. When Darci walked around to investigate, she found the tin lying on the floor.

Just as suddenly as the episode had started, it stopped. Daisy settled in her cage, the room returned to its normal temperature, and the atmosphere felt lighter.

What was she in for now?

## Rosehips
## Class handout

If you don't get around to making cuttings from your rosebushes, or if you couldn't bear to dead-head the last pretty blooms, nature has a nice surprise for you. Rosehips! After the withered petals fall off, a pretty berry-sized ball forms, usually red or orange, the fruit of the rose bush. Rosehips are edible and taste sort of like a cross between a crabapple and a plum. They have a bunch of nutritional benefits, including being packed with way more vitamin C than your average orange. Just don't wait too long before you harvest your rosehips, though, because birds think they're quite tasty and might beat you to them.

**Harvesting**: The best time to collect them is after the first frost, which helps sweeten the fruit. The rosehips should still be colorful and firm, so don't pick any that are shriveled. They can be used fresh or dried, deseeded or whole, but the seeds have a sort of hairy coating you'll need to remove before you pop the rosehip into your mouth. Trim off the stem and blossom ends, cut in half, and scoop out the seeds.

**Drying:** Put the rosehips in a paper bag. You can take the seeds out first or leave them whole. Shake the bag each day to keep the hips from sticking together. When they are completely dry, usually in about ten days, store them in a glass jar.

**Uses:** There are many medicinal uses for rosehips, since they have anti-inflammatory properties. They're used to treat wounds, stiff joints, arthritis, urinary tract disorders, and their anti-oxidants help protect against certain types of cancer and cardiovascular disease.

Rosehips make delicious jelly, syrup, and sauces. For rosehip tea, simply pour a cup of boiling water over six fresh hips, or one teaspoon dried, and steep for about fifteen minutes. Since rosehip tea is easy to find in most grocery stores, you might want to pick up a box and give it a try.

# Chapter Six

*And some can pot begonias and some can*
*bud a rose,*
*And some are hardly fit to trust with anything*
*that grows.*
~ Rudyard Kipling

Darci dropped by to see Max Monday morning. She'd texted earlier to let him know she had something she wanted to discuss with him.

"Mornin' Darci." Max motioned for Darci to follow him to his office. "I'm afraid to ask and I truly dread the answer, but what is this so called wonderful idea you want to run past me?"

His secretary set two steaming coffee mugs in front of them. Darci placed the box of fresh Krispy Kremes she'd picked up on the way over in the middle of his desk and opened the lid. She snagged one and took a bite of delicious chocolate glazed pastry to fortify herself for what she was about to say, sort of like a cowboy downed a shot of whiskey before a gun fight.

"Donut," she mumbled through her full mouth. She gestured toward the Krispy Kremes like a game show hostess. A sugar rush might put Max in a better state of mind to consider what she was about to lay out for him.

"Sure, thanks." He reached for a donut shaped like a football. "Now quit plying me with caffeine and sweets and spill it."

He knew her so well. She flashed back to when she was fifteen and had asked Max to help her convince her mom to let her skip school so she could wait in line to buy tickets for some boy band concert. He'd hidden his grin behind his hand, politely declined, then told her he planned to call the principal each day for the following week to make sure her music-loving behind was parked at her school desk.

She hoped this went better than that.

"Okay, Donovan and I went shopping for out-fits to wear to Stetson Clydell's campaign party, so we got to talking—"

"How in the world did he rope you into going to that?" Max swallowed the bite in his mouth. "Last I remember, you couldn't stand to be around him. Good thing, considering he thought long and hard about having you locked up for tres-passing on his property and harassing his peck-erwood of a dad."

"Believe me, I'm not thrilled about it," Darci said. "Wade's making me go with him. Anyway, me and Donovan got to talking about the break-ins. He's still pretty rattled about his hair salon

74

getting robbed, jumps every time the phone rings or a drawer slams. You got any leads on that yet?"

"Unfortunately, no." Max frowned. "The finger-prints we lifted from the cash drawers don't match any in the databases we ran 'em through. Without eye witnesses, we're not able to make much progress. You can tell Donovan all the pawn shops around here have been alerted to let us know if anybody tries to hock his stolen mer-chandise."

"I'll let him know." Darci cleared her throat. "Well, you see, we kind of had this idea that since my flower shop hasn't been hit yet, that *just maybe* you might want to use it as bait?" When Max opened his mouth to holler at her, Darci put up a silencing hand and used her sweetest smile. "Wait, just hear me out, please. I'm not hiking off through the woods with a shovel or hiding in the bushes with Donovan so we can jump out and throw a net over the burglars."

"It certainly wouldn't surprise me if y'all did." Max calmed himself down, sat back in his chair. "Fine, tell me this cockamamie notion so you can get it out of your system. But," he added, index finger pointed straight at her. "Don't you even think about putting yourself in harm's way to help me crack this case. You got me?"

"Yes sir." Darci's face grew warm. She had to remind herself she was a grown woman now with a good idea, not a teenage kid about to get bawled out.

"Okay, go ahead and I'll listen." Max was all

ears, his tone not matching the gruffness of his earlier words.

"Here's the deal." Darci took a deep breath and tried not to blither out the ideas. "This burglar seems to be set on making the rounds here in Webster County, hitting places that'll be empty at night, businesses that don't make big deposits every day but keep cash in the till. Are we right on that point?"

"Yep." It was obvious Max didn't plan on telling her any details he didn't have to, lest she run out and buy a Batgirl suit.

"Well, the deal with using Petal Pushers is simple and safe. All we have to do is bait the trap with a phony story about there being a reason for me to have a large amount of cash at the flower shop. I don't know, like a fundraiser for charity or something." Darci thought for a second, then had an idea. "The hurricane that hit the Carolinas! I could start a fund to help the victims. Celia Kemp could run an article about it in the paper, we'll post fliers, do a radio spot, get the word out." Darci studied him to see if he was considering it, but he had spit-shined his poker face.

"Great way to make yourself a target," Max said, his paternal nature taking over. "What if they knock you over the head when you're getting in your car, or do a home invasion at your place some night when you're helping Paxton with his homework? Y'all think about that during your brainstorming session?"

"Um, no." The image of masked gunmen busting down her door while her child was home scared her to death. "But you said yourself, they like to hit places without people. In and out jobs where they won't run into any resistance, or armed proprietors."

"Always a first time for everything." Max motioned for her to continue. "But so far, you're right."

"Our plan is this. We put out the word about a pile of cash being raised at the shop on a particular day. Then you and a couple of your deputies stake out the place and nab the guys when they break in!" Her chest swelled with pride over the wonderful plan she and Donovan had figured out all by themselves. "The best part is you don't have to wait in a surveillance van across the street. You can get comfortable in the room upstairs, take turns napping on the daybed." She hated to speak the next words. "So? What do you think?"

"I think you two watch way too much TV." But he grinned. "Good thing you don't think we need a surveillance van, because where in the world do you think we'd come up with one? Unless you want me to use Cole's baby monitor and hide in the back of your delivery van."

He laughed, but straightened up when he noticed the hurt expression on Darci's face.

"You hate our plan." Darci felt like an idiot. She was determined to help everyone involved, and this had seemed like the best way to do it.

"Now I didn't say that." Max leaned forward in his seat and slurped his coffee. "It's actually a pretty fair idea, so long as you and Donovan don't plan to sit upstairs with us. No, you two would have to stay far away from the action, keep the whole thing a secret. And you, young lady, would have to agree to let Carl tail along behind you while the operation takes place. *If* I decide to do it. The deputy would follow you and sit outside your house in his car, not," Max snickered a little. He couldn't help it. "Not in a fancy surveillance vehicle. But he'd stay close enough to ensure that nobody gets near you or your family. That clear?"

"Crystal." Darci was so happy that their idea was a possible go. Even though insurance had reimbursed Donovan for the damages from the break-in, that was nothing compared to the peace of mind having the thugs responsible apprehended would give him. Darci didn't even want to think about having Petal Pushers broken into for real. She also knew the burden of the crime wave weighed heavily on Max, even if he didn't want to admit it.

Back at the shop later that afternoon, Mrs. Jenkins came in to buy a plant to hang in her dining room. Darci shot the breeze with her favorite customer for a while, then had Hoyt walk the elderly lady home with her new spider plant. Odds were good that she'd forget to water it or burn the leaves in direct sunlight.

Darci sat down at the computer behind the counter, clicked the mouse, and watched as the monitor came to life. Her animated desktop featured a cute bee that buzzed from flower to flower in a Monet-inspired wildflower meadow.

She reached into her purse to get the invitation, the pretentious weight of the over-priced stationary evident under her fingertips. Her eyes narrowed to squinted peepholes as she took the card out of the envelope and read over it again. She'd promised Wade that she would RSVP today, to let them know they would be in attendance. Whether she wanted to or not, and she definitely did not.

Her voice sing-songed as she read part of it aloud. "'Stetson Clydell humbly requests your presence'.... Ha! Humble, my Aunt Edith's fanny."

There was a website she was supposed to RSVP through. At least she didn't have to call the jerk in person, or his wife, Phoebe, who thought Darci was a stark raving lunatic. She typed in the URL and pushed enter.

"Oh. My. Freakin'. God."

The screen showed a ridiculous close-up of Stetson, a near rapturous expression on his face, a campaign button held up next to his cheek, his other hand busy making the thumbs up sign. An American flag filled all the space behind him; it was actually waving. Thank God the picture of Stetson wasn't animated. A sound bite played "I'm Proud to be an American" by Alabama. Darci's mouse glided over the screen but could not find an off button to click, so she hit mute instead. Buttons on the bottom of the page read:

ABOUT STETSON!, UPCOMING APPEARANCES!, POLITICAL ISSUES!, DONATIONS!, and finally RSVP!

Darci was torn between laughing and gagging.

A cold spot settled over the room. The invitation fluttered off the desk and directly into the garbage can, even though the wastebasket sat about a foot to the right of where the envelope should have landed.

"Don't blame you, Miss Addie. I can't stand him either."

*Maybe I can figure out how to tell Darci something with that fancy typewriter she's always a-using. Darn thing doesn't have a place to put paper, far as I can tell. Prints the words on that little television on the desk. For all the good that'll do. How in the world is a person supposed to send a letter off to somebody if it's stuck inside a dang TV? Don't make a lick of sense to me. Like those funny lookin' little square boxes folks walk around with nowadays. Call 'em sale phones but I swany, they look like play toys whether they got a bargain on the things or not. Don't have any way to dial 'em, there's no receiver to yack into or hear the other person with, and cain't nobody tell me those telephones actually work, since there's not even a cord to connect 'em into the wall. What a ridiculous way to waste time, if you ask me.*

*Now, let's see if I cain't use this newfangled typewriter. Clydell better not even think about stoppin' me.*

Darci clicked the RSVP! button and rolled her eyes. She hoped a plain page would come up, minus the pomp and circumstance, without any more pictures of Stetson.

"What the heck?"

Darci leaned forward, closer to the now blank monitor. For some reason, the internet had closed. The desktop image didn't even show up, just a blank green screen.

Darci practiced the advanced expertise she had in dealing with computers. She pushed the off button, waited thirty seconds, and then fired it back up. This usually fixed frozen screens and small glitches, and it was safer than whacking the side of it.

The PC booted up just fine.

"Okay then." Relieved, Darci returned to the ridiculous Clydell page.

Just as she hovered her mouse over the RSVP button, the browser disappeared again. This time her desktop showed, but Word opened in a smaller window. She tried to close the word processor, but the mouse no longer worked.

The blinking cursor held her attention. Her hands pulled away from the keyboard. She looked down, but nothing was pushing the keys, even though letters were forming on the screen.

Was this some kind of virus? She hoped not, since she didn't want to have to drop a couple hundred bucks to get the hard drive cleaned and all that mumbo jumbo.

A 'C' and then an 'L' appeared, then a space followed rapidly by two more 'L's. The cursor jumped to the next line and spit out a 'G' and a few more letters.

"Charlotte!" She had to show her cousin this. She wasn't sure what was happening, but she sure as hell didn't need the added stress. "You gotta come take a look at this."

Charlotte trotted up front brandishing a very sharp pair of scissors and a broom handle.

"You okay, Darce?" Charlotte scanned the room, makeshift weapons still at the ready.

"I'm so glad we don't keep an Uzi in the shop." Darci shook her head and tried not to grin. "Put down your weapons and get your butt over here."

"Hey, with all the burglaries, you can't blame a girl for being too careful." Charlotte visibly relaxed.

"You've got a point." Darci felt like a jerk for upsetting her cousin. "Sorry, didn't mean to scare you."

"Scare me, my sweet ass." Charlotte twirled the broom handle and pointed the scissors toward the front door, Ninja style. "Just wanted a chance to show off my moves, go all Catwoman on those burglars."

"Um, I think Catwoman was on their side. A bad guy." Paxton and Jake had dragged her to enough Batman movies that she was pretty sure she was right. "Nevermind that." She pointed to the computer screen and filled her in on everything that had happened since her attempt to respond to the invitation. "Help me figure out what the heck this is all about? Think we're being hacked?"

"Only a moron would waste time hacking into a flower shop." Charlotte studied the screen as a 'T' and a 'Y' appeared. She tested out the mouse for herself but, just as Darci had explained, it was not working. "Freaky."

The Word document showed:

```
C  L   LL
UI TY
```

"Did you try turning it off and on?" Charlotte asked.

"Didn't work." Darci fidgeted with the scissors Charlotte had set down by the keyboard, listening to the swishing sound they made as the blades opened and closed.

"Let me try." Charlotte pushed the control, alt, and delete buttons at the same time. She repeated this like a crazed person banging out some weird three-note chord on a piano. "Damn. Usually works when mine freezes up." Nothing improved, but a new letter popped up beside the others.

Darci started to panic. All the records for Petal Pushers were on the computer. Sales, orders, even her big master to-do list and business budget. The Petal Pushers website was up to date, thank goodness, for now. She'd have to check online orders with her cell phone until the PC got straightened out.

"This has definitely got to be fixed, like now. Do you know anybody to call? This is one thing Wade's wrench can't work on." Darci massaged the top of her head, the spot stress had put in a vise and squeezed tighter by the second.

"Hey, Jimbo might know somebody, come to think of it. Seems like one of his buddies from work fixed his cell phone when it froze up a few months back. Let me call him." She grabbed the phone, the land line from the desk. When Jimbo answered, Charlotte told him about their latest catastrophe, then jotted something down on a notepad.

"So who's our guy?" Darci asked when Charlotte hung up the phone.

"They call him Butter Bean, why I really don't even want to know, and Jimbo says he's a computer whiz. Self-taught, but he moonlights over at Computer Bytes when they get overloaded, so he knows his stuff."

"Great! Give him a call and see if he can do a rush job, which my cheap self will gladly pay extra for."

"Well, that's the part you're not gonna be thrilled with," Charlotte said as she tore the name, number, and information she'd just jotted down off the notepad and pinned it to the corkboard mounted above the desk. "Jimbo says Butter Bean is working the day shift this week so he won't be able to take our call until after four o'clock this afternoon."

"That figures." Darci pinched the bridge of her nose, trying to acupressure the tension headache that pounded inside her skull. It didn't work.

"But Jimbo said you'll love his prices. Cheap." Charlotte grinned, a tiny movement at the corner

84

of her mouth that instantly put Darci more at ease. "We're supposed to tell him who we are, that Jimbo said to give us a good deal, and his fee should only be a fraction of what the big stores charge. Plus he can do it fast, and since he's doing this on the side, no tax."

"That's good news. Okay," Darci said, sucking it up to deal with the situation. "So we'll just have to wait til this afternoon to call . . . did you really say his name was Butter Bean?" She glanced at Charlotte, who nodded through a grimace. "Anyway, with any luck he'll let me drop it off this evening. Bad thing is, now I'll have to call that jerk Clydell and respond to the stupid invitation, and have to listen to him talk. Yeah, sucks to be me."

The temperature plummeted. The ladies saw their breath as they looked at each other.

The bells on the front door jingled even though the door had not been opened.

The next thing Darci knew, Charlotte had turned pale, her finger pointed toward the monitor. "Look at that."

The screen turned from green to a vibrant red, the letters now a sickly neon lime shade.

The missing spaces had been filled in, the last 'L' appearing while they stared at the cursor.

**CLYDELL**

**GUILTY**

As they watched, exclamation marks ran rampant across the computer screen.

"I don't get it." Darci realized that it said something about her state of mind that communicating with a ghost didn't freak her out anymore. "I mean, I agree that Stetson Clydell is guilty of being a jerk. I'm only going to his shindig because Wade insists it would make us look rude if we didn't."

"I'm guessing Miss Addie thinks Stetson is the burglar." Charlotte warmed her arms by rubbing them as she glanced around the room. "No offense, Miss Addie, but I think you may be a little off on this one. That dude has plenty of money stashed away, plus all the cash he's raking in on campaign donations. Can't really see him committing petty larceny and making off with a few curling irons."

The tin box slid from its place on the counter and clattered to the floor, narrowly missing Charlotte's foot.

"Sorry!" Charlotte stepped closer to Darci and whispered behind her hand. "Wonder if ghosts can go senile?"

"No idea," Darci whispered back. Charlotte was right about there being no chance of Stetson going into the cat burglar business. The thing was, Miss Addie usually kept her facts straight, as far as Darci could tell. "But she's trying to tell us something. I just have no idea what it is."

Noise behind them made them spin around to face the computer again. Now the word 'GUILTY' was underlined. And it pulsated.

"Can you be more specific?" Darci said to the ghost, addressing the empty space behind her where she sensed a presence. "What do you think Clydell is guilty of?"

The cursor positioned itself directly under the word guilty. An 'M' appeared.

The computer emitted a series of beeps before the screen went completely dead. Smoke billowed out the sides.

# Petal Pushers Plant Profile for Spider Plant

## *Chlorophytum comosum*
### Perennial houseplant

Spider plants are also called airplane plants.

**Brief description:** This fast growing houseplant has long narrow variegated leaves and produces white flowers and baby plantlets. They're very easy to grow and propagate.

**Trivia:** Spider plants reduce indoor air pollution.

**Growing instructions:** This is one of the easiest houseplants to grow. They need indirect light, but keep them out of the full sun or they'll burn. The fun thing about spider plants is that they produce a bunch of baby plants that are a breeze to propagate. All you have to do is snip the 'babies' off when they have roots and put them in their own pots, or set them in water until they grow roots if they haven't developed any yet.

**Uses:** Spider plants are beautiful in hanging baskets.

# Chapter Seven

*Against a dark sky all flowers look like fireworks.*
*There is something strange about them,*
*at once vivid and secret, like flowers*
*traced in fire in the phantasmal garden of a witch.*
~ G.K. Chesterton

Guests at Clydell Manor filled every room on the first floor and spilled out onto the front porch and patio. Half the people in attendance were Webster County natives. Politicians from around the country mingled with minor local celebrities, including the weatherman and a B-movie actress married to the mayor's grandson. Dressed in formal black and white uniforms, the wait staff flowed through the crowd doling out champagne and tasty finger food skewered with fancy toothpicks Darci could imagine Mrs. Clydell special ordering from Paris. Upbeat elevator music played through unseen speakers. Twinkle lights in the backyard just beyond the patio made the trees in the far corner look much more inviting than the wicker settee she shared with Donovan.

"Can you believe the cleavage that New England senator's wife is letting hang out?" Donovan rolled his eyes and nibbled his canape. "If the wind blows too hard, those babies are gonna pop out right in the governor's face." He wiggled his eyebrows up and down as he fumbled with his smartphone. "I'll get this thing set up to record video, just in case Celia's camera crew misses it. Plus, I'll be ready for your big moment in the spotlight."

"Don't even remind me that's coming up." Darci snagged a bacon-wrapped shrimp from a passing server and took a big bite.

"Swallow that, then we need to get some shots of us for our websites, Facebook, and you know I like to tweet."

They took dual selfies in the grand entryway, then moved to pose in front of the fireplace. They'd only had one cocktail apiece to loosen up, but the faces they made probably had some of the other guests wondering if they were schnookered. Duckfaces, cheek to cheek toothy grins, and a few imitations of their host and hostess looking snooty, well-to-do, seductive, and in Phoebe Clydell's depiction, constipated. They made sure to include plenty of the Beautiful People beside them and in the background.

Donovan actually made Darci forget her nerves while the camera on his cell phone clicked away. Under normal conditions, Darci would never have let him take so many pictures of her. Donovan's jacket pockets and Darci's evening bag were both loaded to capacity with their business cards; her evening bag was limited on space, so he kept her extras in his inside breast pocket. She was going to stuff them in her bra, but Donovan nearly had a stroke at the idea, reminding her that she was accident prone and didn't need a wardrobe malfunction, or to have people see her digging around in her ta-tas over cocktails.

Stetson obviously planned to get as much PR from this little shindig as he could cram in. With the election just a few short weeks away, plying voters with food and booze was a good move on his part. Schmoozing with the upper crust would get him on the local news and in headlines all over the tristate. Unfortunately for Darci, he'd picked her charitable cause to highlight his magnanimity. Stetson planned to present her with a huge donation for the hurricane fund, in front of reporters, with everyone watching.

Donovan rearranged a stray tendril on Darci's hairdo. He'd done her hair himself and Sally from his salon had worked her magic with a few dozen makeup brushes to get her ready to face the crowd.

Darci hoped she didn't throw up all over Clydell, the silly bastard. It wasn't like she could have refused to accept the check, since the contribution would help a lot of folks rebuild their lives in the wake of the hurricane. She hated to be in the spotlight, and Stetson still rubbed her the wrong way.

When Darci and Donovan mingled their way through the study, they stopped to talk with a trio of women discussing the antique furniture in the room. The ladies tucked business cards in their handbags for Petal Pushers and the Hair Dare Your 'Do Salon as they chit-chatted.

"These paintings are very well done," remarked the lady from Shelbyville. "I do wonder why Mr. Clydell hung two portraits of himself side by side, though."

Her friend chimed in. "I was thinking the same thing." The five of them all turned to face the portraits.

"Well, everyone knows politicians are a bit full of themselves," the third woman commented. "It's not really surprising that he's a little conceited."

Her two original companions darted their eyes around the room to make sure no one important had been offended by the comment. Then they made a hasty exit to hobnob in another room.

"I couldn't agree more," Darci said, amused that someone had voiced an opinion in line with her own. "Think I should go tell them that the one on the left is actually Terrence, Stetson's grandfather?"

"No, it's more fun to let them think Stetson is vain enough to plaster his walls with his own face." Donovan put his hand on his chin as they both gazed at the portraits. "The likeness is uncanny, isn't it?"

"Yep," Darci agreed. "Those ladies didn't notice the names on the plaques underneath. Hard to tell them apart otherwise, except for the differences in the way they combed their hair and their clothes being about half a century apart in fashion."

"I've seen twins who didn't look that much alike." Donovan tilted his head, comparing the two images.

Darci squeezed her eyes shut, her fingers pressed against her temples. "You have any aspirin on you? I've got another one of those awful headaches."

He took a pill box from his pocket, shook out two capsules, and handed her the Excedrin.

Someone who worked for Stetson made an announcement. "Stetson's father is about to present his son with a special gift. Everyone, please, gather around the hearth, but leave plenty of room for the photographers."

"Oh boy. Didn't think he'd be here." Darci knew Charlie Clydell better than she cared to, since he lived in the same retirement home as Mabel and Bernice. "He's liable to have another temper fit and wind up on the news, yelling at people to 'mind their b'ness'. As a matter of fact, that's a great reason for me to steer clear of the old coot, so it won't be me he hollers at." He'd done enough of that a few months back.

Spruced up in a nice suit, Charlie barely resembled the ranting lunatic who'd charged out of Golden Days Retirement Home demanding that Darci stop asking questions about his family. He'd given her an earful then, but tonight he stood tall and proud beside his son, playing the part of a stately elderly gentleman.

Apparently no one in the Clydell clan could resist time in the limelight. Charlie gestured with the small box he held as he spoke to his son and their audience, saying how proud he was that his boy was carrying on their family tradition in politics. Caught off guard, Stetson's face lit up when he opened the jeweler's box, his phony campaign grin replaced by authentic human sentiment.

"It's my grandfather's ring," Stetson said as he held his gift up for the crowd. "Thanks, Dad!" He side hugged his father, then both pointed their mugs at the people with cameras. "I hope it brings me as much luck as it did for him."

"Only fittin' you should have it now, so you can wear it when you win the election, just like Daddy did." Charlie straightened out his arthritic spine to stand a little taller. "You know, I was just a little fella when he had this made, about eight years old, but I'll never forget the fit he pitched when one of the stones fell out. Hadn't had it more than a week, so the jeweler was quick to apologize and replace the ruby."

"Dad, you want to tell these folks the story behind Grandpa Terrence and his lucky streak?" Stetson patted the older man's arm in encouragement before he slid the antique family heirloom on his finger.

Darci stepped a little closer for a better look. The ring was beautifully made, not flashy and pretentious as she'd expected. She wondered how much the three gemstones in the oval setting would cost today, and guessed they were worth enough to pay off a big chunk of her mortgage.

"Daddy bought this ring with money he won from bettin' on the Triple Crown. I know it was 1941 because he wore it that fall," Charlie said, pleased to have a room full of people hanging on his words, "when he was elected State Representative. When Whirlaway won the third race, this was waiting for the last jewel. See there," he said, pointing to the gems that now decorated Stetson's knuckle. "He always said the emerald represented the Kentucky Derby win, the sapphire represents the Preakness Stakes, and the ruby, that's for the Belmont Stakes."

Cameramen captured close-ups of the heirloom. The stones glittered in the light from the flashbulbs.

"He wore it when he won the big election, and on every special occasion I can remember for the rest of his life. He loved braggin' on his big wins, and this was his favorite tale to tell." Was that a real tear glistening in the corner of Charlie's eye? Darci liked this side of Charlie so much better than the one he showed at the retirement home.

Stetson took his spot on the stair landing so everyone could better see and hear his spiel. He thanked his guests for coming, then dove right into his political plans in case any of his guests weren't convinced that he deserved their votes. This was followed by him calling up his politician buddies, all of whom sang his accolades as Darci tried her best not to make gagging sound effects.

"Oh good grief, just kill me now." Darci fidgeted with the toothpick from her last appetizer, then licked bacon residue off her fingers before

Donovan gave her a light smack on the hand to make her stop it. He was right. If her picture made it into the local newspaper, she didn't want to look like she didn't know the difference between a cocktail party and chowing down at KFC.

A gust of wind blew through the room, rustling skirts and gently fluffing random hairdos. The cool air felt good on Darci's skin, since the crowd she stood in seemed a bit too warm, possibly due to all the hot air coming from Stetson's mouth. She turned to see if a storm brewed outside the open veranda doors but couldn't see anything much except the twinkle lights.

"Before your time in the spotlight, with your all time fav State Rep candidate? Never." Donovan used his napkin to fix a lipstick smudge at the corner of her mouth.

"That's right, hon." Wade gave her waist a little squeeze as he and Bradley rejoined them. They had also handed out a few business cards to people admiring the renovations they'd recently done on the mansion. "You look too pretty to duck out early."

A gubernatorial candidate who'd had a wee bit too much to drink nearly toppled off the bottom step after a gushing endorsement for his pal. As the intoxicated man made his way back to the bar, Stetson cleared this throat and signaled for his assistant to bring him something.

"There's nothing more important to me than helping other people through tough times. As it says in Luke, chapter six, verse thirty-eight: Give, and it shall be given unto you; good measure, pressed down, and shaken together, and running over, shall men give into your bosom. For with the same measure that ye mete withal it shall be measured to you again." Stetson took a reverent pause. He squeezed his eyes shut while photogs snapped pictures aimed at getting votes from the devout.

"Oh my God. Stetson quoting scripture makes about as much sense as putting Pepé Le Pew on a perfume bottle."

"Darci Shelton," Stetson said, "could you please join me up here?"

The crowd clapped as Darci felt both Wade and Donovan give her a little nudge to get her moving. She would rather get a root canal than go stand beside Stetson, but she exchanged her grimace for a forced grin and hoped no one could hear her teeth grind.

Prone to clumsiness and not wanting to stumble over the stairs like a few other speakers had, Darci reached for the handrail on her way join her host on the landing. When her hand touched the polished wooden banister, it instantly reminded her of the splinter she'd gotten from the rail in her cellar, which made it even harder to keep a pleasant expression on her face. The apples of her cheeks ached as she took her place.

"Darci is a prime example of folks who go out of their way to help their fellow man through tough times. Right after Hurricane Hannibal hit, she set out to raise money to help the victims in the Carolinas who'd lost their homes and livelihoods to the storm. She's taking up donations, running sales in her flower shop to add to it, and has a bake sale scheduled for this coming Wednesday to raise more money." Darci's skin actually crawled when he put his arm around her and gave her a side hug. She spotted Donovan pointing to his own exaggerated grin and renewed her effort to smile and stop flinching.

A loud pop sounded. Glass tinkled to the floor.

Darci flinched and then froze, her mind flashing back to that August morning a year ago, the day she got the tiny scar on her forehead when Roy Nolan took a shot at her.

A few security guards stepped forward. They retreated when Stetson shook his head and pointed toward the high ceiling.

"Nothing to worry about, folks," Stetson said. "It looks like I need to replace some faulty bulbs in Grandma Camilla's chandelier."

Two more bulbs exploded, one after the other. While two maids hurried in to clean up the mess with dustpans, someone had the good sense to flip the switch off before any of the guests caught a chunk of glass in the eye.

"Darci, I want to present you with this check for three thousand dollars, made out to your hurricane fund." His assistant hoisted a piece of cardboard the size of a billboard over the railing to Stetson. It seemed to keep getting caught on something, since they dropped it three times before the politician got a good hold on it. Of course he wouldn't just hand her a regular check. No, he took advantage of the paps as he positioned the ginormous check between himself and Darci and once again grabbed her around the shoulders. Flashes went off throughout the room. Darci's cheeks throbbed from her effort to look happy to be there.

"Oh, my word!" The exclamation came from the middle of the crowd. Darci located an older lady scoffing at the New England senator's wife, the one Donovan had pointed out to her earlier.

Darci swallowed a giggled and hid her expression behind her hand when she saw what caused the uproar. Mrs. New England's dress had actually given away, though she still hadn't noticed it, apparently. Her boobs, in all their silicone glory, were on full display, the fabric from her bodice hanging open to her waist. The politician's wife even smiled pretty for the cameras turned in her direction. Oblivious to her topless state until her husband whipped off his dinner jacket and draped it over her nudity, she was hardly mortified and seemed to rather enjoy the attention as her husband guided her out of the room.

Miffed to have the attention taken off him, Stetson's voiced boomed above the din as he made his way down the stairs. "Attention everybody. That's okay, accidents happen, but let's not embarrass the poor girl. Let's move on out to the backyard, where I've got a little surprise in the form of a fireworks display."

## Trashy Houseplants
## Class handout

Since fall and winter weather limits outside gardening, this lesson shows you how to grow houseplants from things you would ordinarily throw away. You'll need potting soil and decorative containers for these trashy houseplants. Unless you live in a tropical climate far away from my Kentucky home, these plants probably won't produce fruit, but they'll look great in your windowsill.

**Lemon seeds**
These make cute plants that smell nice and citrusy. In a pretty container filled with potting soil, push your seeds into the soil. Water them regularly and set in a sunny window.

**Avocado pits**
The next time you make a batch of guacamole, save the avocado pit. It's okay if you knick it a little when you cut the avocado in half, so don't worry. Wash it off, then you're going to use four toothpicks to hold it partially submerged in water until it roots. Poke the toothpicks in evenly around the center of the pit, pointy end up, then place it in a shallow dish or ramekin with water

in it. Set it in a sunny spot and change the water every few days. It'll take three or four weeks, but then your pit will split open with roots shooting out of the bottom and leaves through the top. Let it grow for a couple of weeks, pinching off the top when the stem reaches six inches. Plant it in a pot with the top half of the pit exposed.

**Pineapple tops**
This grows into an awesome tropical looking plant, and it couldn't be easier. Cut the top off your delicious pineapple, set it in potting soil, then give it a little twist. Put it in a sunny window, water, and watch it grow.

**Bonus: Free Green Onions**
After you cut off the green tops to cook with, save those white ends to regrow your own green onions. Leave the roots on the bulb end, stand them in a glass jar with enough water in it to cover the root section, and set the jar in a sunny window. New green tops will grow to replace the ones you've already eaten. Change the water every now and then, and keep harvesting your frugal crop of green onions.

# Chapter Eight

*The flower that follows the sun does so even
in cloudy days.*
~ Robert Leighton

The computer came back working just fine. Jimbo's friend had replaced part of the hard drive
that got fried, but he was able to save most of the
data. Lucky for Darci that she printed out finan-
cial records at the end of each month, so nothing
vital was lost.

Darci read through the invoice. The repairman
thought a power surge was responsible for the
major damage, and he didn't find any viruses.

The next afternoon, Darci read over the
handouts for her gardening class before she filled
out an order for floral supplies. Her indecisive-
ness over which thickness of wire to get and how
many vases she needed stretched what should
have been a ten-minute job into an hour-long
task.

The computer beeped to her left. Odd, since she hadn't touched it in a while and it had been in sleep mode.

Word was open. She hadn't used it in days, not since she'd worked on the fliers for the bake sale. She slid her chair to the PC to see what was going on, though she had a pretty good idea. Daisy twittered in her cage.

Letters appeared on the screen. All caps, just like the last time Miss Addie had hacked her computer. Darci checked the keyboard and mouse and then under the desk to make sure she wasn't being punked, but all looked the same as it always did.

MURDER slowly spelled across the monitor. Below that, in a font that filled the bottom half of the screen, WATCH OUT!!! pulsated in bold red lettering.

Darci called Charlotte up front. Neither of them knew what to make of the latest message.

"Remember that she typed 'Clydell guilty' last time, and just an 'M' before the computer farted smoke. Well, I guess Miss Addie thinks that Stetson is not only guilty of the being a jerk, but that now he's a murderer. And that we should stay away from him." Darci exhaled, though she was visibly shaken, and confused. "Do you think she believes he'd try to hurt us? I mean, sure, I can't stand the goober, but I can't picture him as dangerous."

"Hey, you need to take this with a grain of salt, or a shot of tequila, whichever you're in the mood for." Charlotte could tell how upset Darci was, and Darci knew she'd produce a fifth of booze with any encouragement. "Don't forget Halloween is coming up. While it might be some cryptic warning from our friendly neighborhood ghost lady, it's just as likely it could be some fool's idea of an elaborate Halloween prank."

"You think?" Darci thought about that, but then shook her head. "But there's a cold spot now, just like the last time the computer grew a mind of its own. No way somebody could fake that."

"But she puts us in deep freeze mode whenever Stetson is mentioned." Charlotte rubbed her arms to warm off the current cold blast chilling her to the bone. "Just sayin'."

"Of great, just what I need," Darci said, rubbing her pounding temples. "Another dang headache." She went to the kitchen for a Tylenol.

When she came back up front, the computer was off. And unplugged. Neither she nor Charlotte had touched it.

"Tomorrow's the big day. Call me later if you need a taste tester." Charlotte licked her lips, imagining the delectable treats her cousin would make to bring to the shop the following morning.

"Sure thing. Tell Cole I'm saving him the best peanut butter cookies." Darci was excited about the fundraiser, and using it as a good excuse to chow down on sweets in the name of helping hurricane survivors.

"This bake sale was a great idea," Charlotte said as she helped Darci move what remained of the gourd and pumpkin display to the edge of the room. They needed the extra floor space, and Darci didn't want anybody to fall and break a leg. "You'll help out all those people affected by Hurricane Hannibal, plus we get to scarf down the leftovers. Win win."

"Yep." Darci sighed. "Except for my thighs. Well, we couldn't put the story out there about a charity and then not actually raise money to donate. Would've made me feel bad, and I sure don't need the bad karma. You know what, though? I'm even more excited about Max staking out the place. I hope our plan works."

Everything was already in place. The police couldn't very well sneak surveillance equipment in tomorrow, not with folks swarming into Petal Pushers to finance the hurricane fund through cookies and cupcakes. Max was upstairs testing out cameras focused on the front and back doors. The shop had been closed for an hour, and since he was working inside, no one should be any the wiser. The spy cams were pretty cool and effective, since she hadn't been able to find where they were hidden until Max pointed them out.

When he was done, they all said goodbye for the night. Charlotte and Darci went to their homes to churn out a few pans of baked goods. Luckily, a bunch of their friends had volunteered to bring things as well. Mabel and Bernice were hosting a bake off at the retirement home and promised to bring dozens of assorted desserts and at least one of Liz Campbell's special rum raisin coffee cakes. (Darci wondered how much rum would actually make it into those cakes after Bernice passed the bottle around. Should be a fun night over at Golden Days). Mrs. Jenkins volunteered to bring three lemon meringue pies, Hoyt's mom was sending red velvet cupcakes, Teresa Maldonado was on the list for bourbon balls, and Mae was down for fried apple pies.

At home, Darci let Paxton order a pizza while she made the first double batch of peanut butter cookies. After dinner, she made two trays of chocolate walnut brownies and prayed for enough willpower to get them cut up and individually wrapped without eating them all. She hit the sack a little after midnight, worn out, with only two cookies and a big brownie in her belly.

By nine o'clock the next morning, Petal Pushers was chock-full of baked goods and customers to buy them. Two display tables in the main room across from the counter were filled with mouthwatering baked goods, and extras loaded down the table in the kitchen. Emily Spenser brought in blueberry tarts and left with some of Charlotte's pumpkin spice fudge and a peanut butter cookie for Peanut.

The fancy glass dispenser Darci usually used for picnic lemonade sat in the center of the counter. It could hold three gallons of liquid, but today it held a sizable number of cash donations instead. She'd seeded it with her own money to start things off, and most folks who came in were happy to add to it. All the cash from the bake sale would top it off that evening. How could any self-respecting burglar resist that big ole pile of moolah? Unless thieves succeeded in making off with the bait, she planned to deposit the money in the morning, so it could join Stetson's donation in the hurricane fund.

Only one thing bothered her about the stake out, and that was the possibility of the robbers being armed. Even though Max was a pistol-packing sheriff, she didn't want him to get caught in a standoff with armed gunmen.

The fundraiser turned out to be good for business. Over half the people who came in to help raise funds for hurricane survivors left with potted mums and fall arrangements. The pumpkins and gourds they'd moved along the wall that morning had lessened by half by the time she turned the Petal Pushers sign to 'Closed' that night.

They tidied the shop and divvied up the leftovers. On the counter up front, the glass dispenser stuffed with bake sale cash could easily be seen from the front door and the window on the porch, plus everyone who had passed through during the day definitely knew where it was.

Darci jumped at a knock on the back door, even though it was right on time. She turned off the lights in the back part of the room before she let Max in. The partial dimness hid his silhouette, should anyone have eyes trained on the shop.

"Come on it and make yourselves at home," Darci said to Max and Deputy Bill Samson.

The two men walked into the hall that led to

the kitchen, workroom, and the stairway.

"There's a tray full of ham and cheese sand-wiches in the fridge, a pitcher of sweet tea, and all kinds of spare snack food left over from the bake sale," Darci said. "Fresh sheets are on the day bed upstairs, and there are extra towels in the bathroom, in case y'all want to freshen up before you head out in the morning, if you're still here then."

"You shouldn't have put yourself out, Darci," Max said, even though she thought she'd seen him salivate at the mention of sandwiches. "We're used to sitting in Bill's old Subaru splitting a can of Vienna sausages on our stake outs. This might as well be the Holiday Inn compared to that. Thanks, and we'll be sure to make use of some of the chow, so it doesn't go to waste. Ain't that right, Billy?"

"Sure thing, Max. Much appreciated, Mrs. Shelton."

"Now, you two ladies go on home. No need to tuck us in," Max said with a chuckle.

"Okay." Darci picked up her purse and dug for her car keys. "But you have to promise to call me first thing if you catch the burglars."

"You know I will. And just to make sure you haven't forgot," Max said. "You and your cohorts aren't allowed anywhere near here until opening time in the morning. Carl's going to follow you home and keep watch over your place tonight, so he'll tell me if your little green Bug leaves the driveway."

Darci was the face of innocence, even though

she'd secretly been thinking up excuses to drive by on a midnight run to the ice machine across town.

"That means neither of you two, nor Donovan, either," Max explained. "Wade has better sense that let you nag him into checking on us. And don't think I'm gonna buy it if you have Hoyt come at midnight to look for his iPod or some such nonsense. Got it, Darce?"

"Of course I do. Don't be silly."

*Somebody is in my house!*

*He's got the nerve, whoever he is, to come in here uninvited in the middle of the night. And there he lays, just a-snoring like a bear.*

*Lord have mercy, what in heaven's name must the neighbors think, with a poor ole widow having a strange man shacked up in here? I swany, I'll look like a brazen floozy. No, no, no, he's got to go.*

*The little dog couldn't help me this time.*

*I've been a-buzzing the thingamajig for the last half hour, hopin' somebody would send the police, what with the burglar everybody's been yackin' about upstairs. I'll just have to go after him with the broom, shoo his behind on out of my house.*

*Well, that didn't do a lick of good. Something mighty funny is a-goin' on. My broom went right through him, then he just looked at me and fell back to sleep. Got a good look at him, though, and it turns out he's that lawman who's some relation to Darci.*

*Been meaning to have a long talk with him, so now's as good a time as any. I'll just fill him in on everything that's been going on. Then he can help me right a few wrongs and protect Darci. Just wish this splitting headache would go away so I can concentrate on what I need to do.*

*I declare, where are my manners? I'm about to ask this lawman to do me a favor and here I haven't even offered him as much as a glass of water yet. Dang headache is scrambling my brain. I just hope he's not as hard of hearing as most folks are these days.*

The next morning, Darci was disappointed to wake up with her alarm rather than from a phone call from Max during the night. Either he hadn't wanted to wake her up with good news about the stakeout, or the whole thing had been a bust. Since this was mainly her idea, her gut told her it was the latter. At least she'd helped raise quite a bit of money for the unfortunate people hit hardest by Hurricane Hannibal.

She spotted nothing out of place when she walked into Petal Pushers a few minutes early. Not that she'd wanted to find signs of a struggle, but it would have been great to see an officer interrogating a cuffed robber in the main room, or at least a note from her godfather saying 'We got the son of a bitch!'

Instead, Daisy sat perched on her swing, the charity money still piled high in the glass dis-

111

penser.

With a sigh, Darci headed upstairs to see if Max and Deputy Samson wanted her to whip them up a little breakfast before they headed to the station.

Max sat up with a start when Darci reached the top of the stairs.

"Mornin', sleepyhead." Darci was surprised he wasn't already awake, but guessed he deserved some rest after staying awake most of the night surveilling absolutely nothing in an empty flower shop. She looked around and frowned. "Where's Billy?"

"Hey there, early bird." Max sat up in the day-bed and ran his fingers through his thick salt and pepper hair. "He went on home around midnight. His little boy has the chicken pox so he kept calling to check on him every fifteen minutes. I figured this place would be quieter without him."

Max looked different that morning, oddly skeptical or guarded. She'd known him ever since the day she was born and was pretty sure she'd never seen that strange expression on his face before.

"Something wrong, Max? You feeling okay?" Darci put her hand on his forehead to check for fever. "You've already had the chicken pox, right?"

"Yes, I had that joy of an itching fit when I was a kid, and no, worry wart, I'm not about to keel over." A small grin twisted his lips. "I'm as fit as a fiddle."

"What aren't you telling me?" She was certain something was bothering Max. He looked jittery, not his usual cucumber cool self. "Did they try to break in? I assumed nothing happened since you never called and I found you playing Goldilocks up here."

"No such luck. That little neighbor dog you told me about was outside barking himself silly right after Billy went home, but that was your only trespasser of the night." Max stood up and tucked his shirttail into his pants. "Some lady came and got him a few minutes later. His owner, I'm guessing."

"If it was a hysterical blonde yelling for Peanut, that would be her." Darci smiled. "Sorry the highlight of this sting operation was a runaway Boston terrier. Come on downstairs and let me whip you up some breakfast."

He followed her back downstairs and opted for some of Paxton's cold cereal, saying he could use a sugar rush to keep him awake. Other than that, Max was being a whole lot less talkative than usual, something that did not escape Darci's notice. He put on the coffee while Darci took milk out of the fridge and poured some over his Fruity Pebbles.

"What aren't you telling me? Looks like you've got something on your mind." Powerless against a kitchen full of leftover sweets, Darci bit into one of Mae's fried apple pies, deluding herself that it was the next best thing nutrition wise to fresh fruit. Since dark chocolate contained flavonoids or some such thing that was good for you, she put a brownie on her plate too. The number on the scale hadn't moved down in weeks, but she was pretty sure it would go up a few pounds before all the extra baked goods were out of the way.

"You sure are the most inquisitive person I've ever met," Max said before he shoveled a spoonful of cereal pebbles into his mouth.

"Inquisitive is a much nicer way to call me nosy." Darci poured a dollop of milk into her coffee and watched the white swirl dissolve into a dark latte hue. "Evading a question usually means you're hiding something. Learned that little tidbit on *Law and Order*." She widened her eyes and tried very hard not to smile. "Did you and Billy watch a porno on the TV upstairs?"

"Very funny, young lady. I think you've been hangin' out with Charlotte too long." Max had almost choked on his kiddie cereal. "If you must know, I had some mighty weird dreams last night, which I hadn't planned to bore you with."

Considering the strange prophetic dreams she'd had over the past year, this piqued her interest.

"Tell me about them." Darci leaned forward. The stakeout was a bust, but the dreams could easily compensate for the letdown. She wondered what sort of message was hidden in the dreams. "Dreams are answers to questions we haven't yet figured out how to ask."

"That a Nietzsche quote?"

"Nope." Darci grinned. "Pretty sure it was Mulder from *The X-Files*."

Max frowned at her over his half-empty cereal bowl. "Had no idea you were so all-fired interested in analyzing random dreams." He crunched on a bite the milk had yet to make soggy.

"I just think they're interesting." Darci didn't want to sound overly eager. "Saw a documentary on dream interpretation last month and I've been thinking about writing mine down in a journal." She pulled a face. "So tell me, did you show up to work wearing a scuba suit or something?"

"No, nothing nearly that much fun. Had the equipment rigged up to sound an alarm if anything moved, so I could get a little shut eye and not have to stay awake staring at the monitors all night. Every dang time I dozed off, I thought I heard the buzzer go off. Had to be a dream because the cameras never caught anything out of the ordinary. I even ran the film back around three, just to make sure some kids weren't messing with me."

Hmmm. Darci wondered if a certain bell jingling ghost she knew might have something to do with that.

"You sure you didn't just keep waking up because you were sleeping in an unfamiliar place? Like when you're in a hotel or a friend's house? Did you actually dream about anything specific?"

Max gave a half-hearted chuckle. "Well, yeah. Once I woke up and thought I saw a woman in old-fashioned clothes standing in the doorway at the top of the stairwell. Must have had that yappy little dog on my mind, 'cause in the dream the lady was trying to shoo me out of the house with a broom." He cleared his throat. "Then I woke up and flipped the lights on. Nobody there."

"You sure?"

"Oh yeah. I even ran downstairs to make sure, but nobody was here. Just me startled awake by a silly dream."

"Anything else?"

"No, that's all, I reckon." Max shifted in his seat. "One other thing, but it's kind of weird. You might want to think about having a housekeeper or maid service come in and help you tidy up."

"Maid service? Really? Like this is the Hilton and I could just hang a sign on the knob." Darci waited for the punch line.

"I woke up around three thirty this morning with the strongest craving for strawberry preserves. I could swear I almost tasted it." Max shook his head, that odd look back in his eyes before he blinked it away. "That's not the weirdest part."

"Well?"

"I dreamed I had a piping hot biscuit served up by the same lady I dreamed of earlier. This time she'd traded in her broom for a fancy pink china saucer shaped like a shell. She sliced the biscuit in half and filled it with homemade preserves, just like my grandma used to do for me when I was a little boy." Max grinned at the memory.

"The dishes were shaped like shells, you said?" Darci's heart jumped into her throat, but she tried to hide the emotions before they reached her face. Miss Addie used to have Belleek china designed to look like seashells. Hattie still had a few of the cups and saucers, and once she'd told her about them, Darci looked the pattern up on the internet. She even had a few of the pieces herself, since she'd posted on Petal Pushers' blog that she'd trade a new plant or arrangement for china in that pattern. What were the chances of a grown man who seldom paid attention to what color his plate was having such a vivid dream about strawberry preserves served on china exactly like that owned by Miss Addie Brown?

A cool breeze swept through the room. Darci turned to see if the window was open. It was closed, but she had a pretty good idea where the sudden wind had come from.

"Yeah. But when I woke up, I noticed a piece of paper under my hand." He lifted an eyebrow. "Darce, it was a newspaper clipping of Stetson Clydell. And there was bird shit splattered all over his face."

Darci remembered that she and Charlotte had lined the bottom of Daisy's birdcage with that newspaper page moments before they heard Peanut barking and found him in the cellar. Right before she unearthed the box the dog had inexplicably attempted to dig up.

"My hand was on the floor under the daybed, like I usually sleep, with one arm hanging down. Thought I heard some kind of bell ringing, woke up craving strawberry preserves and hot biscuits," Max said, confused but trying to find humor in the odd situation. "Instead, all I got was an eyeful of Clydell's stupid mug and bird poop on my fingers."

Max had heard the jingle bells ringing on the front door! Darci wondered if the camera footage captured the bells moving on a closed door, or if audio recorded the ringing sound. Turned out there was no audio to go along with the visual, and the bells were about two inches out of camera shot.

Darci reached up to make sure the key from the metal box still hung like a charm on her necklace. It was still there.

There were no two ways about it. Miss Addie was trying her damnedest to tell them something, but Darci didn't have a clue as to what. Biscuits and bird shit. What the hell could that possibly mean?

One big advantage to owning the place you work is that on beautiful days like the one Darci was having, she was free to be outside. The middle of October in Kentucky was absolutely beautiful, with falling leaves in a rainbow of autumn colors. The weather was cooler than usual, some said as an after effect of Hurricane Hannibal. Sunshine seemed to cast a deeper golden glow while the air smelled crisp and fresher during this season, just past the end of summer but before frost set in to kill the greenery.

That afternoon, Darci was happy as a kitty in a catnip field. Couldn't leave all the raking fun to Hoyt. She started in the backyard and worked her way around to the front, where she stood beside a middling-sized pile of leaves, trying to decide whether to bag them up or jump into them when nobody was looking.

Something buzzed near her butt. She swatted at it, thinking a bee or horsefly must have landed on her backside. Her hand thunked against her back pocket, her cell phone inside it set on vibrate.

Jimbo's smiling face took over the screen, a picture she'd taken from his Facebook page. Darci wondered why he was calling on her cell instead of the shop's landline as she tapped the green phone symbol to take the call.

"Hey, Jimbo. How you doing?" She held the phone between her ear and shoulder and raked up a few more leaves.

"I'm fine." Jimbo's voice sounded funny, his usually light tone clouded with seriousness. Darci dropped the rake, stood up straight, and froze in her tracks at his next words. "Don't freak out, but there's been an accident."

"What's wrong? Oh my gosh." Darci's mind jumped from one possible tragedy to the next. "Is Cole hurt? Hurry up and tell me what happened and I'll go get Charlotte." That had to be why he'd called her. So she could be the one to break whatever bad news this was to Charlotte in person. "What happened, and where do I need to take Charlotte?"

"No, no. Take it easy, but Wade had a little boating accident."

"What?!"

"He'll be okay, I'm pretty sure." Panic rang

119

through Jimbo's voice despite his effort to hide it. "But he's in an ambulance on the way to ER."

Her mind raced even as her knees buckled. She sat down hard on the ground, unconsciously rocking back and forth. Wade and Jimbo went fishing on Saturday afternoons. Paxton tagged along most of the time, but luckily he was hanging out at Jake's house today instead of trying out his new catfish bait.

Boats, water . . . . Oh dear God.

## Charlotte's Pumpkin Spice Fudge

*Since Charlotte spends most of her spare time chasing after her fifteen-month-old son, Cole, she came up with this yummy fudge recipe that only takes a few minutes to make in the microwave. Her little boy gives it the thumbs up.*

**Ingredients:**
4 cups of white chocolate chips (about two 12 ounce packages)
1/2 cup smooth peanut butter
2/3 cup pumpkin puree, canned
4 teaspoons pumpkin pie spice
1 teaspoon vanilla
Optional: chopped pecans or black walnuts

**Directions:**
Put the white chocolate chips and peanut butter in a big glass bowl and heat it in the microwave for one minute. Stir, and keep on microwaving it in 30 second intervals until the chips are completely melted. Add the pumpkin pie spice and vanilla, and then stir until smooth. Pour the fudge into an 8x8 inch square pan that you've greased with margarine or butter. If you're using nuts, sprinkle them on top.

Refrigerate until set. Cut into squares. Enjoy!

**Variations:** You can change this up by using different kinds of chips, like dark chocolate or butterscotch. If you have a peanut allergy, you can substitute any kind of nut butter, like almond or cashew.

# Chapter Nine

*After the leaves have fallen, we return*
*To a plain sense of things....*
*It is difficult even to choose the adjective*
*For this blank cold, this sadness without cause.*
~ Wallace Stevens

Darci was up and running for her car as Jimbo spilled the details, trying his best to let her know exactly what had happened without scaring the hell out of her or candy coating reality. When she got to the VW Bug, she remembered her keys were in the shop. She didn't realize she was crying until she spoke to Charlotte and heard her own sobbed words.

"Hold on, you can tell me in the car. Hoyt!" Charlotte yelled out the back door. "Come cover the shop. Wade's been in an accident so I'm driving Darci to the hospital."

Darci didn't argue. She let her cousin drive them to her wounded husband.

"Jimbo said they were out fishing in their usual spot when the boat turned over. Wade was standing up to reel in a big one when they caught a wave and flipped. He got hit on the head, knocked unconscious." Darci cried into a handful of Kleenex, processing the information herself as she rehashed the details. "Jimbo said when he realized Wade was underwater, he managed to find him and haul him out. Thank God you bought him that waterproof OtterBox cell phone case because he dialed 911 and followed the dispatcher's instructions while he waited for the ambulance. Said he got Wade to puke up water and start breathing again—"

Darci lost it. Wade hadn't been breathing, had been near death. That he'd been rushed to the emergency room in an ambulance pointed to the fact that death was still a real possibility, that she could lose the husband she loved so much. Just like she'd lost her dad.

"He's gonna make it, Darce." Charlotte patted her shoulder but didn't slow the car down. Her emergency flashers warned other drivers to get the hell out of her way as they sped down Highway 41-A. "It'll be okay."

"What if he's not?" Darci couldn't help it; her mind flashed back to when she was only thirteen years old. Her mom had sat her down to tell her that her father was dead, drowned in the lake. He'd been away for the weekend on a fishing trip with some of his old college buddies. Her dad's boat capsized in the middle of Kentucky Lake, and it was days before his body was finally recovered. Max hadn't gone on the fishing trip because he was working a major case, something she knew he blamed himself for. As a little girl, Darci had blamed him for a while too. If Max had been there with her dad, she just knew he would have saved him, or at least have made him put on a damn life jacket. Max and Mae had stayed at their house to help Darci and her mom, Mary, through their grief. The house flooded with tears, their lives forever changed by John Dubois's tragic death.

"I can't make it if he dies, like my daddy." Darci wailed, the pain of her father's loss now fresh in her mind, mingled with her anxiety and fear over Wade's condition. She felt like someone had ripped a bandage off her wounded soul, the pain of being a lost little girl missing her father combined with her dread of becoming Wade's grieving widow. Her worst fear stared her straight in the face.

The turn signal click-clacked as Charlotte made a left into the hospital parking lot and circled near the entrance in search of the closest parking spot. "That's like apples and oranges, Wade is gonna be fine." She handed Darci a fresh napkin she kept in the cup holder, within easy reach when she needed to clean up Cole's spit up or spilled juice. "Uncle John was lost in the water for days. From what you've said, Wade was only under a few minutes at most. The medics were there in a flash. He *is* breathing, Darce."

Darci blew her nose on the napkin, then dabbed her eyes with the clean corner. She wasn't about to check her appearance in the visor mirror, but pushed her bangs out of her eyes and took a deep breath.

"I hope you're right." Darci tried to grin at her, but her face contorted with more tears. "Let's go in."

Darci remembered holding her mother's hand as they walked into the funeral home all those years ago. Her father was the first person she'd ever seen in a casket. She remembered the clatter of Mary's heels slowing as they approached the viewing area. Darci had purposely bitten her lip so hard she'd tasted blood, hoping it would wake her up and she'd find herself in bed with only a nightmare to contend with.

That same feeling enveloped her now. She wrung her hands, letting her thumbnail scratch her palms. Didn't work. It neither distracted her nor woke her from a non-existent nightmare.

She tried to get it together before she reached ER. Charlotte told the nurse who they were and gave them Wade's name. One thing made her feel infinitely better. Had the unspeakable happened, if Wade had not made it to the hospital alive or away from the lake without breathing, Max would have been the one to come tell her in person rather than Jimbo giving her a call.

The nurse led them through a door and around a maze of equipment before they got to Wade's room. She had no idea what to expect, how bad a shape he'd be in, and she'd never been so scared in her life. She would have happily faced a room full of spiders and snakes to keep

126

her loved ones safe, but she was helpless against her husband's injuries.

"Wade!" Darci flung herself into his arms, not caring that his hair was still sopping wet from the lake. He sat on the edge of the hospital bed, a blanket draped around his shoulders. No monitors or breathing machines at work to keep him alive. "You scared me to death."

"I'm fine, Darci. Just wet and groggy with one hell of a headache." Wade looked pale, and his voice sounded weak. Cockleburs clung to his britches leg and probably left scratches underneath the denim. Other than that, he appeared to be in remarkable shape for a man who'd nearly drowned.

"They already did x-rays because of the concussion. He was confused when he first came to in the ambulance, but they think he's gonna make it." Jimbo slapped his friend on the back, trying to lighten the situation.

Darci ignored the bad attempt at a joke and hugged Jimbo instead. "What would we have done if you weren't there to pull him out? Thanks for taking care of him."

"Watch it or my new hero status might give me the big head." Jimbo blushed under a big grin.

Darci went back to inspect the goose egg and fresh stitches in Wade's scalp as Charlotte made sure Jimbo had escaped the boating accident unharmed.

Dr. Phelps came in a little later. He shined a small flashlight in both of Wade's eyes, the pupils of which now appeared to be their normal size.

Thanks to Jimbo getting him out of the water so quickly, and from the paramedic's report, the doctor estimated the water he'd inhaled had prevented him from breathing no more than a couple of minutes. The x-ray didn't show any skull fractures, so a concussion was the worst of the head injury.

He kept Wade for observation for a few more hours, to make sure he didn't have any complications. Because of the head injury, Dr. Phelps told him to take it easy the next couple of days, especially since his job included working with power tools. He wrote a prescription to prevent a bacterial infection in his lungs. The nurse gave Darci a stack of papers about symptoms to look out for when someone nearly drowned and had a fishing boat conk them on the noggin, so she had to watch for Wade developing a fever, slurred speech, vomiting, chills, a cough, or any sudden shortness of breath.

Luckily, none of those symptoms arose. Wade wasn't happy about taking time off work to recuperate, but Darci was pretty sure he enjoyed the extra attention. Darci hadn't been able to sleep until he promised he'd start wearing a life jacket on his fishing boat, no matter how stupid it made him feel. They both realized how close he'd come to dying.

Out in the newest and most expensive of the two greenhouses behind Petal Pushers, Darci re-potted a multitude of chrysanthemums in an array of beautiful colors. A breeze blew through the open door, the scent of autumn in the air. The last batch of these flowers had already sold out, so she was eager to put these mums on the front porch. They would look marvelous amidst the remaining pumpkins and squash.

She was about to holler for Hoyt to come help her move them around front, but then she remembered the two little boys in the shop who could most likely use an easy constructive job outside to keep them from getting into trouble. Paxton had invited Jake over to spend the afternoon with him. Since Wade was out doing something—no doubt making up for those two days the doctor had made him sit home to recover from his boating accident—and the burglars were still on the loose, Darci wasn't about to let the boys stay at home alone, no matter how much they griped about it. Both pleaded that they were way too old to need adult supervision, that some kid in their class had actually made enough money babysitting their little cousin that past summer to buy the newest collector's edition of Mortal Kombat.

After washing her hands, which had been black with potting soil, she headed upstairs to get the boys, figuring she'd most likely interrupt a video game showdown or talk of the latest comic book convention due to come to the area. Instead, the activity they were engaged in stopped her dead in her tracks outside the doorway. She backed into the shadows after what she'd seen.

Her first knee-jerk reaction was to run into the room and stop them, but curiosity prompted her to see what would happen next.

"Okay, I think it's all set up, just like in that movie we watched last week." Paxton's voice was full of excitement. "Got the candles arranged, and a hunk of quartz from my rock collection between that and your new board. You have that Ghost Sensor app ready?"

Darci almost trudged in at the mention of candles, but from her vantage point she could see that her son had the good sense—or fear of being grounded for life—to utilize the flameless battery powered candles she used for displays, to keep her calamity-prone self from burning down the shop. She was still undecided about how to handle things, so when Charlotte walked by the foot of the stairs on her way to the bathroom, she caught her attention, shushed her with a finger in front of her lips, and motioned for her to come upstairs to see what was going on.

"Damn straight," Jake said, confident no adults would overhear him cuss. Probably something else Darci and Jake's mom could thank his uncle for influencing. "See, this part shows the EMF, so we'll know if any poltergeists walk through here." Jake poked the screen on his cell. "This box pops up whenever the EVP picks up spirits talking, which would be way cool." He touched the screen again, then set the iPhone beside the Ouija board. "Let's each put two fingers on the planchette and think of some questions to ask. You can go first, if you want."

"Oh my gosh, that's so cute," Charlotte whispered. "They're trying to have a séance." She grinned at the cuteness until she saw Darci blaring her eyes, shaking her head.

"Are you crazy?" Darci whisper shouted. "What if it actually works? All those EMF thingies they're talking about, I've seen that stuff on documentaries. Leave it to Jake to find an app. How do you think a certain bell ringing spook we know and love is going to react?"

"Oh hell." Charlotte grimaced and cast weary eyes down the staircase. "Didn't think about that. Until now."

"What am I gonna do if he finds out this place is haunted? Not by just any old ghost, but one his mom and crazy cousin are friends with. One we've purposely kept hidden from him for almost two years, lest we warp his logical little mind and freak him out." Darci shushed her before she could answer, since the boys were getting things underway.

"Aren't we supposed to say something special," Paxton nearly whispered. "To call the ghosts out?"

"Yeah, that's right," Jake said. "Don't remember exactly what they said in the movie, but I guess we can wing it."

"Okay." Both boys stared at each other for a few seconds, not sure how to proceed. Or maybe they were afraid the situation would turn out as it had in the movie, which still haunted Darci's mind every time she had to open her closet door at night. "Have at it."

"All right." Jake cleared his throat as they re-positioned their fingertips on the pointy piece that sat atop the Ouija board. Darci couldn't remember the last time she'd seen their young faces look so serious. Jake seemed to search for the right words, probably trying to remember key things from all the movies and late-night horror flicks that involved spirit boards. "We call on all the ghosts from the spirit world who can hear us. You can talk to us through the Ouija board, and it should be super fun for all of us."

Paxton nodded his approval, then they both closed their eyes and waited, just like in the movie.

"Is anybody here?" Paxton asked.

Both boys sat perfectly still. Nothing happened.

In the hall outside the doorway, Darci and Charlotte both held their breath as they watched.

"You know," Charlotte whispered beside Darci's ear. "We should've thought of this ourselves. If this actually works, think how much fun we could have talking to Miss Addie through one of those boards. And you would've saved a few bucks if she sent messages through that thing instead of the PC she fried."

"I don't know. Those Ouija boards are supposed to be bad news. From the stuff I've seen on TV, they're magnets for evil spirits and such." Darci gestured with her hand. "Most of that is just made up B.S. to sell movie tickets, sure, but then again, neither of us believed ghosts were actually real before we opened the shop."

"Just for the record," Charlotte said, stealing another peek at the boys, "I seriously hope the whole evil spirit mojo deal is a load of crap. But it would still be uber-cool to chit chat with Miss Addie through it. Just sayin'."

"She does fine on her own, even—"

A ripple of excitement from the next room drew their attention.

"Cool!" Paxton exclaimed. The boys gaped at the iPhone. "The EMF is picking up a surge."

"We have a ghost in the house!" Jake squirmed in his chair in a way that suggested he needed to go to the bathroom. Then their hands jerked.

The planchette now sat on the word 'yes', printed on the board in fancy old-fashioned script. The wide-eyed boys were startled, but grinned from ear to ear.

"Are you a soldier who got killed in the Civil War?" Jake asked. The answer was no to that question. The entity also wasn't a cowboy, bank robber, Native American, or Jack the Ripper.

"At least they would never think to ask if they were dealing with a midwife with a botanical hobby," Charlotte said during Jake's occupational questions.

"They might be moving it themselves," Darci whispered, hoping that was a real possibility. "Not on purpose, but maybe they're concentrating so hard, wanting it to move, they might be nudging it without even knowing it."

"Were you famous when you were alive?" Paxton asked. This time instead of circling beside the 'No', the planchette glided to 'Yes'.

"Are you a movie star?" Jake asked, his voice brimming with excitement until they got another no.

"They didn't have movie stars back in the old days. Maybe this guy just had a bunch of friends and thinks that's what famous means," Paxton reasoned.

"Yeah, didn't think about that." Jake nodded, then he asked, "Has anybody ever been murdered in this house?"

The EMF app jingled. Even from the hall, Darci saw the small screen light up with the biggest surge yet.

"Good one!" Paxton said. All eyes moved back to the planchette, including the ones hiding outside the door.

The game piece seemed to have an inner struggle with that answer. It darted toward the 'Yes', then moved in small jerks back toward the 'No', then finally did a little jig in the center of the board. Eventually, it stopped on a neutral spot.

"What's that supposed to mean?" Jake asked. "You think he killed somebody on accident? Or he could be a murderer trying to decide whether or not to tell the truth."

"Those kids want it to be a bad guy," Charlotte whispered. "Can't really blame 'em."

The planchette raced across the board in quick frenzied jerks under the terrified yet fascinated fingers of the two boys. Jake called out the letters it indicated in the little plastic window and Paxton wrote them down. The Ghost Sensor dinged at their side. The planchette stilled after it was done with the message.

"What's it say, Pax?"

Paxton looked over the letters he'd jotted down. He added a few marks to separate them into words. "It says, 'Deserved to die. Nosey old bitty. Beware eavesdroppers.'"

Jake dropped another expletive.

"Hey, we're not eavesdroppers," Paxton said, panicking a little over the warning. "We invited you to talk to us, remember?"

Darci and Charlotte grabbed each other, both shaken to the core at having been called out by a ghost who definitely was not their beloved Miss Addie.

"I need to make them stop." Darci moved toward the door, but Charlotte jerked her back before the boys saw her.

"No!" Charlotte said in a barely contained whisper. "Are you crazy? This is the only way to find out what Miss Addie and whoever the hell the other ghost is want to tell us. And from the horror movies I remember on the subject, I think they need to finish the ceremony. To, um, make sure they don't piss off the spirits by interrupting them or something."

The app continued to ding and showed bursts of light caused by surges in the magnetic field.

"Yeah," Jake said, his eyes as big as mule turds. "We're all just having fun. What's your name?"

The planchette again struggled in a fit of small jerks, as if it couldn't decide where to go. Then it spelled out 'Not your business'.

135

The iPhone made another distinct sound, different than the one that indicated EMF changes.

"Hey, we've got something on the EVP!" Paxton exclaimed.

Jake poked the little screen, adjusted the sound, and waited. A breathy, hoarse voice that sounded like something between a whisper and a scream from the grave uttered three syllables that turned Darci's blood to ice. The boys played it over a few times but never could understand what the voice said.

"Did he say 'east of hell' or 'infidel'? What do you think?" Jake asked as they strained to decipher the words.

"Maybe," Paxton said, "or could be 'he won't tell.'"

Darci and Charlotte understood them the first time, and then confirmed it on the repeats. The voice had said, "He's Clydell."

The planchette shuddered and jerked under their fingertips, then zig-zagged violently from one side of the board to the other.

"Should we let go?" Paxton asked Jake with a hopeful gleam in his eye. It was obvious this little adventure into the paranormal was about to scare the bejesus out of them both.

Before Jake could answer, the digital flame went out on the battery powered candles. The light that hung over the stairs behind Darci and Charlotte exploded. The fixture hadn't even been turned on.

The iPhone beeped and the screen shut off.

The ghost, one of them, answered the question

of whether or not they should let go of the plan-chette. It flew off the board, across the room, and hit the wall hard enough to make a dent. Flakes of plaster fluttered to the hardwood floor.

The boys ran out of the room, hell-bent for leather. They didn't notice the eavesdroppers in the shadows as they jumped down half the stairs. The back door slammed behind them.

The women followed after them just a little slower, clutching each other like teenage groupies waiting for a rock star to take the stage. Words escaped them until Charlotte managed to say the only thing that summed up what they had just witnessed.

"Holy shit!"

# Petal Pushers Plant Profile for Agrimony

## *Agrimonia eupatoria*
## Perennial

Agrimony is also called Cocklebur, Stickwort, Church Steeples, Burr Marigold, Philanthropos

**Brief description:** Agrimony grows to about three feet tall, with fragrant lemon-scented oval leaves with notches. The leaves are larger toward the bottom of the plant and smaller toward the top. Spikes of tiny yellow flowers bloom from June to September. After the blooms fade, burrs take their place. These are those dang cockleburs that get stuck on your pant legs when you walk through the woods in the fall and winter.

**Trivia:** This herb is believed to ward off evil spirits. Folklore has it that you can put agrimony under your pillow for a deep sound sleep.

**Growing instructions**: Agrimony grows wild in the woods and on the side of the road. In your herb garden, the plants need full to partial sun.

**Uses:** To treat colds, fever, diarrhea, sore throat, and wounds, and as a mouthwash or gargle. It can be made into a yellow dye.

# Chapter Ten

*Wild is the music of autumnal winds*
*Amongst the faded woods.*
~ William Wordsworth

Darci chatted with Suzanne Flemming when she went to the bank to make a deposit and swap some larger bills for small change. The burglars had yet to be caught, so she didn't like to keep any more cash at the shop than was necessary. She and Suzanne were right in the middle of a conversation comparing whose husband was most addicted to ESPN and football games, a sport neither of the ladies took particular joy in watching, when Mel Harper joined them.

"Hey, Mrs. Shelton, I was about to give you a call." He motioned for her to follow him. "If you have the key on you, you're welcome to open the safety deposit box we discussed a few weeks ago. It was delivered this afternoon."

He left her alone in the vaulted room, as was customary, to give her privacy when she opened it. The box was old, she could tell by the design etched on the front panel. She ran her fingers over the top and wondered again what could be inside.

She slipped her necklace over her head, inserted the key into the lock, gave it a twist, and then opened it. A lone envelope was inside the box. She recognized Miss Addie's handwriting from the midwife log, and it was her neat script on the front that spelled out 'To Whom it May Concern.' She stared at the yellowed envelope, trying to decide whether she should open it there at the bank or take it back to the shop and wait until Hattie could be with her. But her friend had been adamant that she should read it and the letters—which hadn't contained anything out of the ordinary—and let her know what was in them.

Curiosity got the better of her. Darci opened the seal and took out a folded sheet of paper.

She read the document, and let out a gasp.

*To Whom It May Concern,*

*I'm writing this document in hopes no one other than myself will ever read it. The lives of my dearest friends, as well as my own, are in jeopardy. If you're holding this page, then the worst has already happened. If I turn up dead, I am hoping this paper will bring the man responsible to justice and keep him from killing anyone else. He's had blood on his hands for many years, probably from more crimes than I'm aware of.*

*Since I have no way of knowing how things will play out, and for fear of this page falling into the bloody hands I mentioned, I'm only going to give my friend's first name, Betsy. My daughter Virginia knows how to get in touch with her (but has absolutely no idea about the things I'm about to divulge in this document), should authorities need to find her to keep her safe from the man who caused her so much pain and took so much away from her. For this same reason, I must be vague on some of the details.*

*Betsy recently discovered that her daughters were named beneficiaries in a will that was enacted some years ago. She fears for their lives and her own should they ever come back to Webster County, and made me promise I wouldn't confront the man myself, a promise my conscious wouldn't let me keep. The person who stands in the way of the girls' inheritance is also the man who murdered their father.*

*I witnessed the murder in 1905. The deepest regret of my life is not going to the authorities back then. It would have been impossible, given the cir-*

cumstances. I helped Betsy and her daughters escape his evil clutches and swore that I'd take her secret to the grave with me in order to keep her family safe. But that was before she learned about the will.

I went to this man last week. He believed Betsy and her daughters were long dead and was none too happy when I told him they were alive and kicking, and showed him a photograph to prove it. Though the girls were infants the last time he saw them, there is no mistaking who they are in the picture. Now he knows that I saw him shoot Betsy's husband. I told him I'd keep quiet about all that if he passes the inheritance, which he is in control of as executor of the will, on to the rightful heirs. This is a very wealthy man in need of nothing, except my silence on the matter. He said he'd get the money to me in a few days so I can take it to my friend, in exchange for my continued silence on the matter.

From the fire in his eyes and the things he said when I first approached him, I don't believe him. I feel in my heart that he means to shut me up for good, and would do the same to Betsy and her daughters if he ever found them.

The man I fear, the man who shot

*his own brother in cold blood, is none other than Terrence Clydell. I assured him that if he fails to keep his word, I will tell everybody who'll listen all about what I saw him do. His being a murderer would surely put a damper on his election hopes.*

*May heaven help us all.*

*Sincerely,*
*Adelaide Brown*

Darci called Hattie as soon as she made it back home after work that evening. She hated to be the bearer of bad news, especially since Hattie hadn't felt well lately, but she had no right to withhold this information from Addie's grand-daughter. It didn't prove Terrence Clydell had actually hurt Addie, though that was a real possibility, but it contradicted facts concerning who had shot Ellis all those years ago.

The choice of not calling from Petal Pushers was simple, since she didn't want to upset her resident ghost by rehashing the details within her earshot.

Charlie Clydell, Terrence's son, had told Stetson that it was his grandfather, Titus, who accidentally shot Ellis. Terrence had been in his early teens at the time, and the story was that he and his dad Titus had only meant to send Betsy and

144

her twins away. The gun had gone off when Ellis came in and caught them threatening his wife. Whether Charlie had been lied to or changed the facts around, she had no idea.

"Never in a million years did I expect something like this to turn up." Hattie was outraged rather than hurt after Darci read the document to her. "I guess this explains why she hid the tin in the cellar."

"You're right, it does. She must have been scared Terrence would find the letters with Betsy's return address, and find out where she lived. As well as the alias she'd been living under all that time."

"But that's not all. Remember how Ellis' name in Grandma's midwife log was crossed out, but in a different type of ink? We all thought it was strange since it looked like she'd came back years later and blackened it out. Guess she must have done that after she talked to Mr. Clydell." Hattie paused, and Darci pictured her pacing around her living room. "Never thought it would be a blessing that Grandma fell down those stairs, before anybody got a chance to hurt her.

Darci wasn't so sure about that. An accidental fall was the best case scenario, but there was a real possibility she'd been pushed down those stairs. There were some other things that needed to be factored in, and Darci thought it best to play devil's advocate without focusing too much on the murder aspect with her elderly friend.

"Hattie, please don't take this the wrong way," Darci said, hoping what she was fixing to say wouldn't hurt Hattie's feeling. "Miss Addie was getting on in years when she wrote about all this. Do you think she might have, well, sort of confused some of the facts? Like mixing up Terrence and his dad, Titus? Or that she could've been a teensy bit paranoid about one of the Clydell's wanting to kill her?"

"Anything's possible, I suppose. Grandma had all her wits about her, best I can remember, but I was just six the last time I saw her." Hattie thought for a few seconds. "Whether it was Terrence or Titus who killed Ellis, we'll never know for sure, but I do remember something. Didn't you tell me Stetson mentioned a woman who showed up and tried to claim the inheritance years ago?"

"Hattie, your memory is better than mine," Darci said. "I'd forgot all about that, but you're right. That's exactly what Stetson said Charlie told him."

"Well, dear, that nosey old woman he mentioned had to be Grandma, considering what she wrote in that document." Hattie was as sharp as a tack despite being eighty years old. "That proves she really did contact the Clydells. I guess it was best that she died from tripping down the steps when she did, before Terrence could get his hands on her, if that's really what he'd been inclined to do. Don't guess we'll ever know what his intentions were."

Since there was no way to discern what really happened down in the cellar, they would both sleep better believing it was simply a terrible accident. Darci prayed Hattie was right.

"Don't you boys dare run off where we can't see you." Darci would never be able to find Paxton and Jake if they got separated in this crowd. Hundreds of people filled the street and they hadn't even got to the festival yet. Wade bellyached about forking over six bucks to park almost a mile away, but Darci could count the walk to and from the car as exercise. Her yoga mat hadn't seen much use these past few weeks.

The West Side Nut Club Fall Festival in Evansville, Indiana, is one of the largest street fairs in the country, second only to Mardi Gras. Each October, Franklin Street closes down to traffic for one week as vendors set up along each side to sell a vast variety of food that ranged from ordinary to exotic. Profits from the food booths and carnival rides go to local charities and non-profit organizations in the area. It was a pretty big deal so local news crews covered it every day, showing footage at noon and six p.m. to encourage people to come out and join the fun.

Paxton's favorite part was the rides, so their first stop was at the ticket booth. Wade volunteered to accompany the boys on rides Darci totally refused to get on, like the pirate ship that rocked so high she could barely look at without puking. He promised to take her on the Ferris wheel later. She wasted no time hitting up the food booths until time for them to all meet back up in front of the vendor who sold fried pickles with marinara sauce.

Music played through speakers as she passed a stage set up in the middle of the culinary chaos. A crowd of hungry people on a heartburn crusade roamed the street, rowdy teenagers ran amuck, and frantic parents chased after little kids on sensory overload.

After perusing her Munchie Map, she decided to start the afternoon's culinary adventure with something at least halfway healthy. A catfish sandwich filled the bill, a huge one that was bigger than the bun, dressed with pickles, onion, and the perfect amount of hot sauce to set her tongue a-tingle. She savored every delicious bite.

So much had been on her mind lately, this outing was just what Darci needed. She hadn't even objected when Wade asked her to leave Petal Pushers a few hours early, so they'd have plenty of time to enjoy the rides, sample the food, and play carnival games. It worried her that Hattie was still getting over some kind of bug when Darci called to read her Miss Addie's document concerning Terrence Clydell. It was old news, literally, but she knew it hurt Hattie to find out someone had held a grudge against her grandmother. Darci planned to call and check in with her in a few days, just to make sure she was all right.

The caramel apple stand was next on her list, but she got sidetracked by the smell of deep-fried chocolate chip cookie dough.

"Yes please," she answered when the vendor

asked her if she wanted powdered sugar on the five big clumps of fried gooeyness. "And plenty of chocolate syrup."

Darci bit into the first piece, closed her eyes, and moaned in ecstasy as the flavors combined on her taste buds.

She grabbed a can of RC on her way to the apple stand. Fruit on a stick coated with a few layers of flavor counted as a guilt-free heart healthy treat in her book. She opted for the caramel apple dipped in chocolate, drizzled with peanut butter, and rolled in crushed pecans.

It was tricky to walk and eat at the same time. With her mouth crammed full of caramel coated fruit, she bumped into a lady eating a turkey leg. To make matters worse, Darci accidentally spit bits of chewed apple in her face when she tried to apologize. They shrugged at each other, and Darci decided to sit on the curb until she ate the rest of the apple down to the core.

Halloween decorations loomed everywhere. A man in a cheesy ghost costume hawked pumpkin spice apple cider to the crowd. Unfortunately, seeing him brought another of Darci's worries to the surface, one she tried to push out of her mind as she searched for a trash can to toss her apple stick into. She hoped the second ghost who'd turned up at the flower shop wouldn't stick around. Quite frankly, it scared the hell out of her. Miss Addie was a vital part of Petal Pushers, an old friend who just happened to be invisible and brought cold spots wherever she went. This other entity, though, it was pure evil. It busted

light bulbs, made threats and threw the planchette during the boys' séance, and jerked the
key on Darci's neck with enough force to leave a
mark.

Part of her hoped Hoyt was just playing an
elaborate Halloween prank, but she doubted it,
unless he was taking a college course on the fine
art of tormenting the hell out of people. Besides
that or a lurking spirit, burglars trying to scare
her off to make their job easier was the only other
logical explanation she could think of, but that
just didn't make sense. Donovan didn't experience anything out of the ordinary before they
knocked over his hair salon, and why would anyone waste the effort?

Darci shivered at the memory of the voice
picked up by the EVP, which had to be Miss Addie saying the other ghost was Clydell. But which
one had she meant? She and Charlotte had assumed the Ghost Lady was still on her kick of
blaming everything on Stetson. After reading the
document from the safety deposit box, it seemed
more likely that she'd meant Terrence, or possibly Titus if she was still confused about who shot
Ellis all those years ago. But there was no reason
for any of the Clydells to suddenly decide to
haunt the flower shop, since neither had lived
nor died at Petal Pushers. Maybe the Ouija board
summoned a random entity with an agenda of its
own.

Enough with the worries. Determined not to
think about anything else unpleasant, she
grabbed a corn dog to nibble on as she strolled

around taking in the sights.

Paxton and Jake were starving by the time Darci met back up with them and Wade. The sun had just gone down and even more people clogged the roadway. She absolutely refused to let them get brain sandwiches, one of the hot ticket items though she could not for the life of her figure out why anybody in their right mind wanted to eat, well, a mind. Whether it came from a cow or pig, she didn't know and wasn't about to ask. The sight of the thing was almost enough to make her turn vegetarian, if not for the maple bacon cooking in the next food truck.

They parked the boys at a picnic table with their corn dogs and funnel cakes, ordered them not to move one inch away from there, threw in an 'or else' for good measure, and then Darci and Wade stood in line to ride their favorite attraction.

The Ferris wheel was so tall, it dwarfed even the highest steeple of the historic Saint Boniface Catholic Church. The view from the top was absolutely incredible. Lights illuminated the crowd below, as well as buildings between the Ferris wheel and the Ohio River. Had the circumstances of Wade's boating accident been any different, he wouldn't be there with her tonight, a thought that made her treasure these magic moments even more. With Wade's arm around her shoulders, she snuggled closer to him, glad it was just the two of them in the swaying car.

"This is the most relaxed I've seen you in a long time." Wade gave her a quick kiss on the cheek. "Glad I dragged you out here?"

"Heck yes," she said, smiling up at him. "All work and no play makes me a little nutso sometimes, but I'm having a blast tonight. It was nice of Charlotte to work until closing for me, but I don't think she minded."

"You know she didn't. That girl loves to play boss lady when you're out of the shop." Wade shushed her when she objected to the job title.

Flashing blue lights and sirens roared down the street and came to a screeching halt in front of Petal Pushers. Max darted out of the car and joined Darci on the front porch while deputies Samson and Smith ran around back.

"They're probably long gone, but we'll check it out," Max said, one hand on his service revolver and the other on the door knob. "You wait right there, just in case."

The store was a ransacked mess when Darci went in that morning. She'd unlocked the front door, but immediately noticed the back door standing wide open and broken glass on the floor. From the looks of it, somebody had one hell of a good time knocking stuff off tables and busting things up.

Her heart stopped. She had to check on Daisy but was scared to death of what she might find.

As she took a deep breath to steady herself, the parakeet tweeted. The cage still sat on its shelf behind the counter, and she'd never been so happy to hear the little bird sing. Other than being a little puffed up from the breeze coming through the open door, Daisy was perfectly fine.

Darci had nudged the back door closed with her foot so the bird wouldn't get chilled from the cool morning air. Then she'd went out on the porch to call Max and text Charlotte, so she wouldn't freak out when she pulled into work and found police cars in the driveway. Darci didn't want to touch anything on the crime scene or smear any fingerprints the burglars might have left, but she was itching to clean up the mess. She dreaded finding out exactly how much had been stolen. At least she had insurance on the store that covered theft, accidents, fire and flood, and most acts of nature, thanks to a lesson learned that spring when her expensive uninsured greenhouse was ruined in a storm before she'd added it to her policy.

"All clear, Darce. Come on in." Max held the door open for her.

Her godfather was in full sheriff mode as they walked through each room. He jotted down all the missing items and noted the damages. The cash register was gone, along with all the money inside it. The only other thing that had been stolen was the copper tubing she'd ordered for Charlotte to make into wreaths.

Charlotte helped clean up the rest of the morning, and Hoyt went to work fixing the back door, replacing the busted lock. The place was a total mess, but there wasn't much damage other than glass and potting soil scattered from when the burglars threw plants around the main room. By noon, they were able to open for business, with Charlotte in charge while Darci drove to town to buy a new register and stop at the bank for money to put in the till. Hopefully, any customers that came in before she returned would either have exact change or pay with a check or credit card.

The stolen items and damage amounted to about fifteen hundred dollars. Insurance should cover most of that, minus the deductible. Darci had scrimped and saved and watched every penny, and it hurt that she'd have to be out any money now, especially since she was still struggling to try to pay off the cost of replacing the greenhouse. Things could've turned out much worse. Nobody got hurt and no real damage was done, but she felt violated. As the day wore on, anger set in. Too bad the thieves hadn't made their move on Petal Pushers during the stakeout. And too bad Miss Addie hadn't been about to run them out with her broom handle.

That night, exhausted from spending most her day cleaning up after the burglars, Darci had a terrifying nightmare.

She dreamt that she was at Petal Pushers, but it was set up like a home rather than a flower shop, and looked much the way Hattie had described it from her childhood. The house was hot, despite a breeze through the open windows. It was early morning, she could tell by the way the sunlight painted the far wall.

The canner on the antique stove heated things up even more. Darci didn't feel like herself. Clean dishes dried next to the sink as she finished up making a batch of strawberry preserves. Jar lids pinged on the kitchen counter. When the timer buzzed, she took the rest of the jars out of the canner and placed them on a layer of towels to cool.

She jumped at a loud bang, the sound of the front door slamming shut. It hadn't been locked, not during daylight in her safe small town, and she didn't expect any visitors for a few days.

Darci hurried to the living room to find out who was in her house. It looked strange to see her workspace changed into a living area. She spotted a marble top table under the porthole window, an orchid on top beside two other potted plants. Furniture that dated back to the twenties or thirties filled the cozy room. There was no television, but a large old-fashioned radio was positioned next to a rocking chair.

"Hello," she said, caution edging into her voice. "Who's there?"

Someone spoke behind her. Her skirt twirled as she turned around to confront the silhouette of a man. She couldn't make out what he was saying or see his face. Things happened all at once and made no sense. The room spun as the man approached her. She backed away even as she tried to stand her ground. Terror churned her stomach with each step she retreated.

155

The room grew dim, as if a dark cloud had entered the house. The man raised his hand, an object clutched in his fist. The worst pain she'd ever felt echoed through her skull as she fell back hard against the wall and crumpled to the floor. Broken shards of china rained down. They were pieces of Miss Addie's beloved Belleek plate.

These were the same pieces Wade had found when he fixed the hole in the wall, the ones Darci had turned into a mosaic clock. A glance at the wall showed a fresh hole where her knee had made contact with the drywall.

The man swung at her again. Before the object in his hand crashed into her head, she cried out. The blow reverberated through her skull as she landed face down on the floor, on top of plaster fragments and broken china. The world went dark but for a few specks of light as she lost consciousness. The sensation of being dragged and then hefted were the last things she remembered when she woke up screaming.

She ran to the bathroom and barely made it to the toilet before she threw up.

## Miss Addie's Strawberry Preserves

*This makes about three and a half pints of the best strawberry preserves I've ever had. Hattie Delaney gave me her grandmother's recipe and a few jars to sample.*

**Ingredients:**
8 cups strawberries
Fresh lemon, zested and squeezed
5 cups sugar

**Directions:**
Wash the strawberries and cut off the tops. Put the berries in a large heavy pan and crush slightly with a fork or the bottom of a jar. Add the sugar, two tablespoons of fresh squeezed lemon juice, and your desired amount of zest. Stir together and bring to a boil. Cook over medium heat until the preserves thicken and become transparent. Take the pan off the heat and skim off any foam. Ladle into sterilized jars and process in a water bath canner for 10 minutes.

# Chapter Eleven

*The world is tired, the year is old,*
*The faded leaves are glad to die.*
~ Sara Teasdale

Darci decided to call Hattie, to see if she was feeling any better. A bulb shipment came in that morning that included some tulips bulbs she planned to surprise Hattie with, since she'd mentioned how much she liked the ruffled parrot variety.

It was a beautiful fall morning, crisp temperature in the fifties, sunshine streaming down in a beautiful golden glow that seemed to kiss the trees and evergreens. She took her cell out back and relaxed on the bench under the big oak tree. A gentle breeze played with her hair as she pushed the call button under Hattie's picture. Birds chirped in the limbs above her while she waited for Hattie's cheerful voice to answer the phone.

"Um, hello."

"Oh, uh, sorry," Darci said, startled by the unexpected squeaky masculine voice that answered. "I think I must have misdialed."

"Not if you're calling Hattie Delaney," the young man on the other end of the phone replied. "This is her phone. I'm her grandson."

"Oh, she's mentioned you," Darci said. "You must be the one who helped her move those boxes in from storage a few months ago. And you taught her how to send emails and tweets. Seth, right?"

"Yep, that's me." She thought she heard the teenager sniffle, as if he were choking up.

"Is your grandma around? This is Darci Shelton, from the flower shop in Dixon that used to belong to your great-great-grandparents."

"Um, no, she's . . . ." Definitely choked up now, the boy struggled audibly to finish the sentence. "Grandma is in the hospital. Want me to try to give her a message?"

"Oh my gosh, what's wrong? She mentioned she hadn't been feeling well, but I hope it's nothing serious." Darci talked way too quickly when flustered, and that she was. "Is she alright?"

"Well, mom said she should be okay . . . if everything goes well." The boy took a deep breath. "She had a heart attack last night. Woke Granddad up after midnight saying there was pressure squeezing her chest, and her jaw hurt . . . in ICU now . . . stable, the doctor said."

Darci couldn't stand to hear the pain in the

boy's voice. Her eyes welled up as she imagined an older Paxton coping with a similar situation. She wished she could give the kid a big hug and some reassurance, but she was scared to death. Hattie was every bit of eighty years old. Darci sent up a silent prayer before she could say anything else to Seth. She wouldn't have time to make the two-hour drive before visiting hours were over or she would've jumped in the car en route to Clarksville, Tennessee.

"Your granddad still doesn't believe in carrying a smartphone, does he?" Hattie had rolled her eyes when she'd told her about the way Gene just didn't take to newfangled technology.

"Nope."

"Didn't think so. I'll call the hospital and talk to him." Before she hung up, Darci added, "Don't worry, I'm sure your grandma will be fine."

Max swung by Petal Pushers a few days later. Ever since the burglars hit the flower shop, he'd made a point of checking in on Darci every couple of days, hoping his squad car parked out front so often might safeguard against the crooks coming back.

"Be with you in a minute, Max." Darci was helping Paxton's bus driver pick out a new fall wreath to hang on her front door. "Got a fresh box of Krispy Kremes in the kitchen, if you want to go help yourself to a couple. I've got dibs on the one with chocolate sprinkles, though."

161

He returned to the main room nibbling on a donut as Darci made change for the customer, a pretty brunette wearing a *Dukes of Hazzard* T-shirt. He held the door open for her, since she carried a big wreath in her arms.

"I'm guessing that's her car?" Max grinned at Darci as the bus driver made her way around the pumpkins and down the porch steps. "The big orange Dodge Charger that matches her shirt?"

"Yep, and I'm gonna beg her to take me for a ride the next time she comes in." Darci opened the front door and waved. The horn tooted "Dixie" as the car pulled away from the curb.

Darci and Max were still talking about the ba-dass car when his portable beeped. He stepped out of the room talking to dispatch through the speaker mic. He returned without the stoic expression he usually wore when called out for an official emergency.

"Good news." He wasn't in too terribly big of a hurry to leave, since he took the time to drain the rest of his coffee and wrap up the uneaten half of his donut in a napkin to take with him. "Looks like the burglars got themselves caught red-handed last night. Two deputies are bringing 'em in, so I'm off to meet them at the county lock-up."

"Now?" Darci wasn't an expert on police procedure, but the order of events confused her. "It's almost nine o'clock in the morning, so if your men made an arrest last night, how come they're just now getting around to bringing them in?" Her imagination took off as she pictured Deputy Samson in a shootout with a couple of guys wearing ski masks. "Everybody okay? Did they put up much of a fight?"

"Nope." Max popped a donut hole in his mouth, a grin on his face as he chewed knowing full well that curiosity was about to get the best of Darci. "The perps almost ran to the squad car by the time my boys got there, after they cut off the zip ties." His eyes twinkled as he watched Darci's reaction. "Funny story behind it."

Patience was not her strong point, especially in official business she wanted to poke her nose in.

"Well?" Darci set down her coffee mug, freeing her fingers to fidget with her napkin. "What happened? You know you're killing me here."

"Don't want a homicide on my hands. Too much paperwork." He winked, and she blared her eyes at him. Then he let out a belly laugh and explained the situation. "Emmett Patton from the pawn shop across town has one hell of a nice security system set up. He lives a few doors down from his store, so he's rigged it so an alert comes directly to his cell instead of the security company, since he's a do-it-yourself hands-on kind of guy. Last night when Jimmy Fallon was going off, Emmett got an alert. He grabbed his ball bat and a shotgun before he ran over to put a stop to it."

"Um, that was over eight hours ago," Darci pointed out.

"Yep. Turns out a couple of teenagers are behind the crime spree." Max stopped to chuckle again. "From the sound of the way ole Emmett dealt with 'em, I'll be surprised if they didn't piss their pants. Them being young and stupid is the only thing that saved Patton from going upside their heads with that Louisville Slugger of his. He waited til sunup to call the station, and when Samson got to the scene, he found two eighteen-year-olds tied to chairs in the middle of the room. Emmett spent the night showing them all the guns and hunting knives he had in the store, explaining all kinds of creative ways he could utilize them against dumbasses who tried to rob him."

"Good move! No matter how much time they get for the burglaries, I bet they won't ever forget Emmett's lesson." Darci was relieved they'd been caught. She was also thankful she'd raised Paxton in a way where she was pretty darn sure he'd never think about doing anything as stupid as robbing a pawn shop.

"The one kid was still crying when he climbed in the car, thanking Samson for saving his life. The other one kept telling Emmett how sorry he was and that they'd never bother him again." Max looked at his watch and headed for the door, his napkin wrapped bear claw still in his hand. "Gotta go. Can't wait to hear the rest of the details when I get there. Just hate to see young men screwing up their lives like this."

Hoyt knew one of the burglars from high school, though they hadn't ran in the same social circles. Tommy Hinkerman was the boy who'd set streamers on fire at last year's homecoming dance. Darci guessed she and the rest of the businesses they hit were lucky Tommy hadn't torched their buildings after he stole what he wanted. After Max interrogated the young men, it was easy to see why the stakeout at Petal Pushers hadn't worked. They didn't have a method to their break-ins, no master plan, but just drove around chugging Budweisers until they spotted a place likely to have cash in the drawer and no alarm. Hinkerman and his friend, Paul Simms, were sentenced to a year in the county jail and ordered to perform a whole lot of community service to make up for what they'd done. Darci figured she'd see them in orange jumpsuits, picking up trash from the side of the road. She felt bad for their parents and hoped the young men could turn their lives around by the time they got out, but the punishment fit the crime.

Darci looked like warmed over cat poo as she stood by the porthole window sipping coffee. Each morning she liked to take in the view, clear her mind, and savor a little peace before her day got too chaotic. She had a few minutes before the shop opened and hoped to feel a caffeine jolt strong enough to keep her awake through the busy day. At least her headache was better, thanks to the extra strength Tylenol she'd popped. After one more glance at the blue sky through the nearly bare branches of the oak trees, Darci took a deep soothing breath, just like her yoga DVDs had taught her, then exhaled on her way to the counter.

After waking up a little past three a.m. from a nightmare, she'd been too rattled to go back to sleep. By the time Wade and Paxton came down-stairs to get ready to go to work and school, she'd done three loads of laundry, cleaned out the fridge, and made a huge breakfast bonanza for them complete with bacon, eggs, waffles, fruit salad, and fresh squeezed orange juice.

The images she'd seen in her sleep left her horrified. There was always the chance that it was simply a bad dream brought on by too many horror movies. She realized that. The most likely explanation was that her imagination had run wild after she read Miss Addie's document about her fear that Terrence had it in for her. A few months ago she'd had another series of dreams that turned out to have been a message from be-yond, complete with flashbacks to 1905 and hints about where a body was hidden. Since Dar-ci had actually dug up that particular corpse, she'd have to be pretty dense not to figure out the ghost had something to do with some of the im-ages that popped into her slumbering mind.

That's what was scaring her. She hoped her imagination was to blame for this last nightmare, which was pretty awful. Like the one she'd had last week, it started off with her in the kitchen at Petal Pushers making preserves when someone slammed the front door to the shop. Only the building was a home again instead of a store, one furnished with things from the era Addie Brown had lived there. A mysterious man appeared be-hind her each time in the dream. He spoke, but she couldn't make out what he said or see what he looked like. Then he'd hit her over the head with something. She'd slammed into the wall before being bludgeoned in the head again. The blows caused unbelievable pain, a migraine-level headache that stayed with her after she'd woken up.

This one ended with Darci unconscious in the dream, with the sensation of being dragged and then picked up. She'd come to, in the dream, slung over the man's shoulder like a sack of potatoes as he carried her down the cellar steps. Her hand jutted out to grab the railing. She'd clawed at the wooden banister but couldn't get a hold even though she felt wood embed under her breaking fingernails. She tried to punch and kick the man, but her injuries and the position he carried her in hindered her efforts. Her assailant threw her down the rest of the stairs.

She'd heard her own bones crunch and break as she bounced to the bottom. She laid there cold and numb but for her throbbing head. As she slipped into the unconsciousness of death, she heard glass shatter all around her. As if bludgeoning her and then tossing her down the stairs wasn't enough, the man was throwing her fresh preserves at her as she lay there dying. The sticky red strawberries oozed out around the glass shards even as her own life drained from her dream body.

Darci sipped from her third cup of joe when Charlotte got to work.

"Happy Halloween!"

Darci nearly spit coffee across the room. After she quit choking and coughing into her napkin, she stared at her enthusiastic cousin. "What the hell are you supposed to be?"

"Pizza Rat, can't you tell?" Charlotte pointed at the foam pizza on the front of her costume, then at the pointy plastic ears sticking up out of her short blonde hair. "Remember the YouTube about the subway rat making off with a slice of cheese pizza? Well, ta da! Whipped it up myself."

Charlotte wore a tiny gray skirt with fake pizza and tail attached, matching tee and tights, and cute black combat boots with silver zippers and a buckle. She twirled around a few times to show off her ensemble.

"I forgot you were going to dress up." Darci gave her the thumbs up. "Cute. Good luck not catching a cold in that barely there skirt when you're out trick-or-treating with little Cole to-night."

"Hey, it's not that short." Charlotte twirled again and flashed a sarcastic smirk. "You should be happy I didn't go with my first choice, which I would've, except I didn't want Hoyt hanging out in the workroom all day, Instagramming pics of me in a Lady Godiva outfit."

"Sad thing is, I know you're serious." Darci gave her a half-grin and shook her head. "Glad you went with the R-rated mouse."

"I'm a rat, but you're welcome very much." Charlotte took the seat beside Darci, careful to hold her tail to the side as she sat down. "What's the matter, Darce? You don't look too festive on my favorite holiday."

"Just tired." She decided not to bog Charlotte

down with her depressing dream when she looked so happy. "Stayed up reading late and didn't get much sleep before my alarm went off at the crack of dawn. I'll be fine after a few deep yoga breaths." Darci closed her eyes, inhaled a cleansing breath through her nose, and then exhaled through her mouth.

"You want me to light you a candle?" Charlotte's eyes danced as she watched her. "Chant *ohm*, bang a gong, set a little ambiance for whatever the hell you're doing?"

"Ha ha, very funny." Darci raised an eyebrow in her cousin's direction. "I'm trying to stay calm, center myself, crap like that." She took another deep breath. "See, it's helping already."

"If you stand on your head or strike one of those weird poses, you know I'm gonna put a picture of you doing it on Facebook."

"The only weird pose I'm tempted to pull right now would be mooning you." Darci grinned, but her crossed arms. "By the way, if I ever find a funny little picture like that of me on the internet anywhere, I think I'll just have to post that pic I took of you in college. The one from that night in old man Fletcher's pumpkin patch."

"You would not dare." The cousins exchanged glares, Darci with another raised brow, Charlotte with a mock sneer.

"Oh yes I would, with a big goofy smile on my face." Darci tapped a forefinger against her still throbbing temple. "Anybody who thinks a picture of me advancing my health with a yoga pose is funny would absolutely keel over laughing at you, drunk off your rocker, sipping Jack Daniels by the pale moonlight. I believe I've still got that particular snapshot in my scrapbook. One of my favs. The one where you used two miniature pumpkins and a corncob to make that scarecrow anatomically correct."

"You were three sheets to the wind yourself." Charlotte pointed her finger at Darci. "I do remember that much from that night. Fell down laughing your ass off."

"Yeah, because it was hilarious. You sang that Cheap Trick song, "I Want You to Want Me", while you worked your glue gun." Darci loved having the upper hand. "And you were twerking around that scarecrow way before it was called that." She was having so much fun picking on Charlotte, she almost forgot about her headache. "Wish we could've seen Mr. Fletcher's face the next morning. Don't think I forgot where you left that whiskey bottle."

"You know," Charlotte said, crossing her legs and leaning back in her chair. "I could whip up a real funny display for the front yard. A real show stopper that would give kids something funny to ask their folks about. Might do that after lunch."

"Like hell you will." Darci pushed her cousin's leg and sent her spinning around in her office chair. "Over my dead body."

After she put the 'Closed' sign in the window that evening, Darci went down to the cellar to

look for the motion activated skull Paxton asked her to bring home. She'd bought the Halloween decoration for the shop, but the stupid thing was just too annoying, with its red flashing eye sockets and that maniacal cackle. It'd lasted one day before it landed on Darci's last nerve, thanks in part to Hoyt setting it off every two seconds. That's when she'd banished the thing to the depths of the cellar.

The willies usually crept up on her when she had to go down to the cellar, and it was worse now, after the horrifying nightmares she'd been having about the place. Plus it was Halloween. But she'd promised Paxton she would bring the dang annoying skull home before he went trick-or-treating, so she'd just have to suck it up and find the thing.

Halfway down the cellar stairs, Darci's whole body began to shake. She switched on the flashlight even though she could see pretty well from the bare bulb swinging overhead and the street lamp that shone through the open doorway. When she reached the bottom, she shined the beam around the boxes of holiday decorations. Five minutes later she knew exactly where all the Christmas balls and plastic Easter eggs were, but she hadn't found the hideous skull.

She'd have to check the boxes under the steps. That was about the only other place it could be. "Please, don't let there be any mice or spiders under there," she said out loud as she bent down to duck walk under the stairs. She gulped and added, "Or anything that slithers. Especially nothing that slithers."

She pulled each box away from the wall to look through them. Why she'd kept so much useless crap, she had no idea. Finally, tucked into an old crock pot container, she found what she was looking for. Good thing there weren't any batteries in it. She definitely would've pissed herself if the motion activated eyes had lit up or that awful canned maniacal laughter poured through the speakers in its ears.

As she pushed the boxes back against the wall one at a time, the flashlight beam glistened off something in the farthest recesses of the darkness. She skooched in further to see what it was. Probably just some old crumpled up tensile, she guessed.

The flashlight went dead.

Great. She'd have to replace the batteries, but she was pretty sure she had some spares in the workroom. At least the single bulb that hung from the ceiling gave a little light. She ran her fingers along the crevice where the wall met the hard packed dirt floor, and prayed she didn't disturb any brown recluses taking a late afternoon snooze. Her fingertips brushed against a small object that had to be the glistener. It felt like a small rock or earring, which made her think it was a piece that fell off the Christmas garland. She closed her fist around it, tucked Paxton's toy skull under her arm, and crawled out from under the stairs. She would definitely need a shower when she got home.

The cellar seemed darker than usual, darker

even than before she'd checked those last boxes. Then she noticed that the cellar door at the top of the stairs was shut. Must have blown to.

Halfway up the stairs, she held up her hand to see what she'd found in the spider haven. The bare bulb overhead made it sparkle. At first she thought it was an earring, due to its shape, but there was no post on the back. She moved to the next step, and froze when she realized what it was.

The light bulb exploded. Broken glass tinkled down onto the crude wooden steps.

The cellar was as dark as the inside of Dracula's coffin.

# Petal Pushers Plant Profile for Tulip

## *Tulipa*
## Perennial bulb

**Brief description:** Tulips are spring blooming perennials that bloom in a plethora of shapes and colors. Tulips are a sign of spring, one of the most popular flowers of all time, and they're easy to grow.

**Trivia:** There are over 3,000 registered varieties of tulips. This flower gets its name from a Turkish word for turban, due to the bloom's shape. Tulips symbolize true love and fame.

**Growing instructions:** Plant tulip bulbs in the fall, at least eight inches deep, four to six inches apart, with the pointy end sticking up. Deadhead tulips after they flower.

**Uses:** Tulips look beautiful in cut arrangements, planted in containers, and growing in rock gardens, borders, and flower beds.

# Chapter Twelve

*By the pricking of my thumbs,*
*Something wicked this way comes.*
*Open, locks,*
*Whoever knocks!*
~ William Shakespeare

Vertigo set in, which only added to her growing panic. Darci's heart beat against her ribcage so hard and so loud, she was sure she was about to have a heart attack. If she didn't get a grip on herself, she was going to fall down the stairs and break her neck.

Images from her nightmares flashed through her mind, the only thing she could see in the pitch blackness in which she now stood. In the dreams, a man had hit her repeatedly over the head until she was unconscious, then brought her to the cellar and threw her down the stairs when she made a grab for the railing.

Miss Addie had fallen down these very stairs to her death. Darci had begun to believe her dreams were a glimpse into the past, an attempt from the other side to right a horrendous wrong. She suspected the ghost had something to do with them, but hoped she was wrong. Adelaide Brown had feared for her own life before she died, positive that Terrence Clydell meant to do her in if he had the chance. Hattie chose to believe her grandmother had simply taken a fatal fall instead.

Now the truth was evident.

Darci held proof in her hand. Her fist held not a piece of Christmas garland or an earring. She held a ruby. In a cut that perfectly matched the replacement in Stetson Clydell's ring.

The hair on the back of her neck stood at attention and a flutter of panic surged through her stomach. She felt a strong presence, would almost swear someone stood on the step beside her, and could literally feel someone's eyes bore into her through the darkness.

It wasn't Miss Addie. Of that, she was certain. Her presence was the polar opposite of whatever ominous being lurked in the cellar. For a second she convinced herself that someone must have hidden in the cellar earlier, to wait for a chance to attack, but that wasn't possible. She'd searched every inch of the root cellar and found no sign of a living person amongst the cobwebs and dust.

The last few minutes of her life replayed in her mind. The found ruby that proved Terrence Clydell a murderer, the door mysteriously shutting on its own, and the bursted light bulb. The last time she'd seen bulbs pop like that was at Stetson's shindig right before . . . right before Charlie presented him with his grandfather's ring, the one which once held the ruby in her hand.

She had to get out of the cellar! If her thinking was correct, that would mean one hell of an evil spirit named Terrence Clydell was there with her, thoroughly pissed off that she'd just found evidence that proved he killed Miss Addie.

Even if she managed to make her way up the stairs without breaking her neck, ole Terrence wasn't likely to let her out. She recalled the day Peanut had been stuck down there, when she and Charlotte had the devil of a time opening the door.

Her foot located the next step up, but her body didn't follow. Maybe she should go back down rather than risk falling or being pushed. There was no doubt now that Terrence had been the entity to yank her necklace hard enough to leave an abrasion around her throat. He'd been after the key that threatened to expose him for the monster he was, a secret he planned to guard even in death. That explained why she'd only felt his presence after she opened the cookie tin. God only knew what else Terrence was responsible for during his lifetime, and capable of in the afterlife. Exactly how much danger she was in, she didn't know and didn't want to find out. During the boys' séance, his ghost had thrown the planchette across the room with enough force to knock a hole in the wall. A ghost with that much strength might be able to heave her down the stairs. Should she feel her way up and push on the door, or go back to the relative safety of the dirt floor and wait for this hellish experience to end?

Indecisive on what to do, she bent her knees, and while tightening her grip on the ruby, shifted her other arm to place the skull on the step. She slid the gruesome decoration to the left, so she wouldn't trip over it if she had to feel her way up the stairs in the dark. Her cell was out of her pocket and in her shaking hand by the time she'd stood back up. The instant the screen lit up she wondered why she hadn't thought to use the flashlight app, but honestly, she'd only been in the dark a few seconds. Her panic just made it feel like forever.

Her contact list held another problem: who to call? Everyone else had left Petal Pushers for the night, so no need to ring the shop phone. Wade would give her a ribbing for being too scared to leave the cellar alone, and Max was all tied up with his investigations, plus all the minor mischief brought on by Halloween. Charlotte lived about ten minutes away, but Darci hated to risk waking Cole up before his pre-trick or treat nap was over. Then again, it would be less trouble for Charlotte to deal with a grumpy baby than have to run the shop full-time if Darci fell and hurt herself bad enough to have to stay in the hospital. There was only one other person who could help her.

"Miss Addie," she said, "I could sure use your help right now, if you can hear me."

Turning her attention back to the phone, she wavered between whether to call Wade or Charlotte to come over and open the door for her. The ruby bit deeper into her palm as her fingertip reached toward Wade's picture on the keypad.

The screen cracked as her index finger hovered over it.

"Shit on a biscuit!" Darci tightened her grip on the smartphone, afraid her shaking hand would drop it. She needed the small amount of light the broken screen still managed to put out.

The phone vibrated. The back grew hot, as hot as if it had been left in an overheated car on a July afternoon. The icons disappeared, the screen turned a strange shade of green, and the cell vibrated one more time. Then it went totally dead.

Dead was not a word she wanted to think about just now. Terror seized Darci in a way it hadn't in years. Even a few months ago when she'd been stuck in a pit with a century old corpse and a copperhead slithering around her feet, she hadn't reached this level of fear. A certain ghostly friend had dropped a rope down right before that happened.

"Help!" Darci squeaked when she heard what sounded like boot heels descending the topmost stairs.

At that second, a familiar cold spot settled around her, cold enough to be evident even in the chilly cellar. Tears of relief filled Darci's eyes. Never before had she so feverishly wished she could hug the ghost who undoubtedly now stood by her side. She wasn't sure exactly how Miss Addie could help her, but she knew the Ghost Lady was her very best shot at making it out of there more alive than Addie had in 1941.

The boot heels sounded again. They couldn't be more than two steps ahead of her now. Fleeting hope of intruders belonging to the footsteps would have been better than this, knowing a murderous ghost was there with her at the scene of his heinous crime.

The door began to shake on its hinges.


*Don't you worry, Darci, I won't let Clydell get you. My head's still a-splittin' from when he threw me down the stairs, but I'm here and not about to leave your side. I'm gonna have to call out my big guns, though. Betsy's here—you remember her from when she dropped that ladder down to you in the pit a while back—and our ace in the hole is on the way. But I promise you, Darci girl, we won't let that monster harm a hair on your head. He'll have to go through me first.*

*Terrence Clydell, you get on out of here! You hear me? You've got hell to pay for what you've done so you'd better ante up. Never been so mad in all my born days, but you know good and well why all this rage is a-bubblin' to the surface. You ought to be ashamed of yourself. Bad enough you shot your own brother in cold blood and tried to kill Betsy and their poor little baby girls. Then you come knock me in the head and throw me in the cellar.*

*Your murder streak ends here. Just you step back and leave her alone.*

*No matter how hard you try, you cain't keep the truth buried forever, thank the good Lord. Turns out you couldn't shut me up either. Your secrets out and there's nary a thing you can do about it.*

The door slowly creaked open. The glow from the light pole in the backyard silhouetted the figure of a man who seemed to struggle to hold it open. Darci couldn't tell whether he was fighting the wind or ghostly forces, and so long as he was going to let her out, it didn't make much difference. She couldn't make out who it was, though there was something familiar about his stance. Wasn't Hoyt or Charlotte, that was for sure.

She was so relieved to have the veil of darkness lifted, she didn't care who it was. The ruby, which she clutched tightly in her fist, bit into her palm from the force of her keeping her fingers closed so she wouldn't drop it. This was not the time for clumsiness.

To her left, in the periphery of her vision, for barely a split second, an apparition in old-fashioned clothes appeared. Miss Addie looked very much as she had in the newspaper clipping she'd found at the library last year. A feeling of equanimity settled around Darci like a cloud of calm on this tumultuous night. Miss Addie was letting her know she was there to protect her.

Something in the room changed, shifted some-

181

how. The scent of burning sage replaced the earthy mustiness. Either a full moon was shining bright enough to cast a dim glow through the cellar, or something else thought they needed light, which further comforted Darci's rattled nerves. Now, with the place lit by some unseen source, she could see her surroundings.

She could almost make out the face of the man who opened the door. Now she knew why he looked so familiar to her, and her heartbeat raced once more.

"Terrence?" God, Darci hoped she was wrong. It didn't make any sense that he'd lock her down there in the first place if he planned to materialize to open the door. Something about his stance screamed Clydell. "Stetson? Who's there?"

If it did turn out to be Stetson, how the heck could she explain why she'd just called out to his long dead grandfather? A trip the loony bin was looking like a very real possibility in her future.

"I cain't believe y'all get those two mixed up." Charlie Clydell shook his head and huffed, then he looked straight at Miss Addie, or at least that's what Darci thought, since his gaze pointed straight at the last spot Darci had seen her a few seconds before. Did he know Miss Addie stood beside her?

Darci felt her jaw drop. How many more surprises could this night possibly hold? Charlie was the very last person on earth she expected to come to her aid. As a matter of fact, he'd made it crystal clear in the past that he wouldn't be bothered to yell for help if her hair caught on fire.

"My dad's nose was a little crooked, but my son's is as straight as a movie star's. And just take a good gander at Stetson's eyes next time you run across him. Got 'em from his mama. Made him softer than the rest of us, but the boy's got a good heart." The old man straightened his spine and stood a little taller, either from pride or maybe he was afraid he'd given away his son's weakness and regretted mentioning Stetson's Achilles heel. "He's a good man and a damn fine politician, so don't you ever forget it."

"Yes sir, Mr. Clydell, I'll remember that," Darci said, her voice so shaky she almost didn't recognize it as her own. "Um, how did you know I was down here?"

"Don't you worry about it, little miss ask too many questions." No doubt about it being Charlie now. The cantankerous old fart.

"Well, um," Darci said, trying hard not to say anything else that would piss him off before she got out of the cellar. "I appreciate you stopping by to help. Thanks." Darci picked up the skull decoration Paxton wanted her to bring home, the object responsible for her being down there in the first place. She wanted to ask Charlie if it was all right for her to leave, to make sure he wasn't there to help his long-dead father commit another murder. Had he known about it? He would've only been a little boy way back in 1941, so it wasn't likely. Surely claiming murder victims wasn't something that came up in father-son conversations.

Charlie ignored her thanks, his mind still on

his family. "My daddy wasn't perfect, but he was the best man I've ever known, regardless. I'm proud to be his son."

Darci knew better than to say one word against Terrence right then, but felt like she was somehow betraying Miss Addie by not setting the record straight about her murderer. Plus Charlie would likely slam the door shut if she did, and plunge her back into the darkness with a homicidal ghost. She hoped he didn't plan to stand there all night trying to convince her about the virtuous character of the Clydell clan. She ventured to take one step up.

Charlie's gaze rested on a point directly in front of Darci. She could make out his eyes in the dim light, but she had no idea what he was looking at so intently. There was no way he could possibly know she held the missing ruby, but if he did, he'd also know how it had wound up in Adelaide Brown's root cellar. He wasn't looking at her fist.

"Well, get a move on. Time now for everybody to clear on out of here." Charlie stepped back and held the door open wide. "Head for home."

Darci wasted no time. A wind brushed past her from the depths of the cellar and blew her hair toward the door. She wondered if it was Miss Addie making a rush toward Charlie, but doubted it. She was pretty sure Addie was sticking close to her. The cold spot clung to her like a comfortable shawl.

The ominous presence, however, seemed to disappear with the rush of wind.

With the echo of each step that clanked against the stairs as she went up, she thought about Miss Addie dying down there, all alone, all those years ago. The scent of sage grew stronger, with the slightest whiff of lemon verbena, as images popped into her mind of Betsy fleeing the cabin after her husband was killed, of her escaping with those two baby girls clutched to her chest, her best friend on her heels. That had been the first link in the century-old chain of events. Addie risked everything to help her friend escape the Clydells, only to have her own life taken by Terrence thirty-nine years later. Now Darci had a very clear understanding of why Stetson was so unwelcome at Petal Pushers. He wore the face of his grandfather, Addie's killer. She was one lady who would not forgive such injustice, against herself or her loved ones, and held the grudge long after her own death.

Darci prayed that somehow, tonight could be the final link.

"See, I'm not as mean as y'all thought, huh," Charlie said, his mouth twisted into a smile bent from years of sarcasm. "Now we can put this behind us, but we'll all be better off if you two just figure out how to mind your own damn b'ness."

With that, Charlie was through the door and gone, out into the foggy darkness.

Darci wondered how he'd make it back to the retirement home on a night like this and started to go after him, offer him a ride. She stopped herself, pretty sure it would only piss him off. Golden Days was only three blocks from the shop, plus he was sure to encounter plenty of trick-or-treaters to yell at on the way. She figured Charlie would make it home safe and sound.

## Darci's Apple Pie Protein Smoothie

*This tastes just like apple pie in a glass, plus it's good for you. The perfect thing to whiz up for a quick breakfast or a healthy afternoon snack.*

**Ingredients:**
1 apple, core removed (Don't bother to peel it, who has the time)
1 banana (you have to peel this)
1 cup almond milk
1/4 tsp pumpkin pie spice
2 TBSP of protein powder
1 or two ice cubes, to make it cold and creamy

**Directions:**
Cut the banana and apple into a few pieces and put them in a blender. Pour in the almond milk, and then add the protein powder and pumpkin pie spice. Pulse a few times to break up the fruit, then add the ice cubes. Pulse a few more times, and then blend until smooth.

Nutrition information: 342 calories, 7 grams of fiber, 65 carbs, 17 grams of protein

# Chapter Thirteen

*Autumn is the mellower season,*
*and what we lose in flowers we more than*
*gain in fruits.*
~ Samuel Butler

Darci was glad the first thing on her to-do list the next morning was a trip to Golden Days Retirement Home. Even walking around the neighborhood while Paxton went trick-or-treating the night before had done little to help ease her jitters from everything that had happened in the cellar.

She hoped Terrence's ghost was gone for good, swept away in that gust of wind shortly after Charlie opened the door. No nightmares had plagued her sleep last night, which was a good sign, and she didn't feel his ominous presence. Still, she imagined it would be a while before she worked up the courage to go back down in the cellar alone. Then she smiled. One thing she was certain of, Miss Addie had her back.

Darci drove her green Volkswagen Beetle to the retirement home and park out front. Armed with her trowels, a planting diagram she'd drawn up days ago, and a bag full of bulbs tucked under her arm, she headed for the benches in the front yard. She could hardly wait to see the assortment of daffodils and tulips in bloom next spring.

She'd just finished covering up the last tulip bulb by the second bench and was fixing to head to the tree Mabel liked to sit under. The new variety of crocus would be perfect blooming in that spot in a few months. Someone called to her before she'd made it two steps in that direction.

"Morning Darci." She recognized Bernice's voice before she'd turned all the way around to greet her favorite residents. Mabel was with her, the two making their way across the lawn to chat.

She could hardly wait to hear the latest gossip that was bound to leak out of Bernice's lipsticked mouth. Mabel spoke first, eager to see what Darci was planting, and ask if there was a chance she'd let her help.

Darci had just finished answering her when she remembered something she was dying to tell them.

"Hey, you're not gonna believe who came to see me last night." Darci set the sack of bulbs down again. "I got myself stuck in the cellar, and the very last person I'd ever expect to help me dropped by out of the blue."

She had no intention of telling the ladies about

the paranormal things that occurred. Only Charlotte got the full scoop on that. She still felt kind of bad for not calling to check to make sure Charlie had made it back safely, but the last thing she'd wanted to do was piss him off by meddling in his "b'ness." She wondered if he'd speak to her cordially the next time their paths crossed, or if he'd revert to the cantankerous attitude he was known for.

"Well, if it was Robert Redford, you dang sure had better have him waiting in your car to meet us!" Bernice slapped her leg and let out a bawdy laugh.

Mabel grinned and shook her head.

"Afraid it wasn't him." Darci wondered exactly what would happen if Bernice got her hands on her celebrity crush. She almost blushed imaging Charlotte and Bernice having that conversation, but shook the thought aside. "I was never so surprised in my life when the door opened and there stood—"

The sight of Stetson Clydell walking out the side door with his shoulders slumped, a box under one arm, and a handkerchief balled up in his hand stopped her cold.

"What's going on with him?" Darci pointed to Stetson as he climbed into his car and blew his nose. "Let me guess. Ole Charlie got up to some kind of grumpy Halloween mischief and he had to come clean it up before word got out." Met with blank stares and an uncharacteristically quiet Bernice, she prodded, "What exactly did the old fart do this time?"

"Um, you're barking up the wrong tree, I'm afraid. You see, Charlie passed away yesterday." Bernice had never got along with Charlie, was actually the one who had started calling him an old fart as a nickname. Now there was solemn reverence in her voice as she spoke. "His boy came to box up some stuff this morning. Been sitting in his room since we went to breakfast."

"Charlie is dead?" Darci could not believe her ears. Guilt tugged at her heart. If she found out Charlie Clydell had fallen ill or gotten in some deadly accident yesterday evening after he'd left the shop, she would never forgive herself. Especially after he'd saved her from an impossibly tough situation. She still had no idea how he'd known she needed help. "Oh my god! Are you sure?"

"Yes," Mabel said. "Never woke up from his nap. May he rest in peace."

"You okay?" Bernice grabbed onto Darci's arm when the world started to spin and she stumbled. "You look kind of sick."

"I . . . it's just terrible news." Darci felt sick to her stomach, and confusion rattled her brain. "Did you say he went in his sleep? No heart attack or accident?"

"Yes, honey, he just passed in his sleep of old age," Bernice said. "Best way to go, if you ask me. He didn't show up for lunch, so they went to check on him, and he was already gone. But don't go gettin' yourself all upset. He lived a long and ornery life and I bet Charlie wouldn't have done things one bit different."

"At lunch!? You sure he died around noon? Yesterday?" There had to be some kind of mistake. Relieved as she was to know the old man hadn't been hit by a car walking back to the assisted living facility, it threw her for one hell of a loop when they mentioned the time. He'd been in her cellar after the shop closed last night. Couldn't have been a minute before six thirty. Bernice had to have the details fuddled up, but that wasn't like her. She might be elderly, but she was as sharp as a tack.

"Around then," Mabel said, her voice less cheerful with the news of a fellow resident passing. Though a stroke had affected her speech and mobility, therapy had worked wonders over the past months. She spoke clearly now, but at a very slow pace. "Ambulance left with his body before bingo started at one."

"But—" Darci had nearly said that was impossible. Then she realized there was only one way it could have happened, and how he'd known she needed saving from Terrence. Not something she thought she should tell her friends. Even if they believed her, they didn't need the shock at their age.

"That's too bad." Darci needed to leave, to go find Charlotte, pour a stiff coffee and Kahlua for each of them, and tell her that it was Charlie Clydell's ghost that saved her from Terrence.

Now it made perfect sense why he could see Miss Addie.

"Oh shoot." Darci made a show of checking her watch. "Don't think I'll have time to get these crocus bulbs in the ground today, but I can finish up next week. I've really got to get back to the shop."

"I can plant those." Mabel eyed the bag with the crocus bulbs. "You know I love to garden."

Darci bit her lip. She hated to leave any job undone, but if she didn't vamoose pretty quick and sort out her thoughts, she was going to burst. There weren't many bulbs left, just a few to set under the big tree in the front, and she knew it would make Mabel's day to get her hands in the soil.

"That would be great, Mabel, if you're sure you don't mind." Darci showed her where she'd planned to set the bulbs and left two trowels, in case Bernice decided to help. Then she hightailed it out of there so fast, her tires squealed.

The maid shut the door to the study after she'd asked them to have a seat and make themselves comfortable. Darci wiped her sweaty palms on her jeans and checked her purse for the fourth time since leaving Petal Pushers. The Altoid box was still there, and rattled when she shook it to prove it wasn't empty.

She nearly jumped out of her skin at the sound of Stetson's footsteps closing in on them.

"You *are* gonna help me explain this, aren't you?" Darci was so grateful Max was there with her. No matter how polite Stetson Clydell treated her, she knew he still thought she was a nut job.

Before he could answer, the door opened. Stetson walked in and shook their hands before he sat down. Darci had done most of the flowers for Charlie's funeral, and Stetson had been nothing but cordial to her in return. She'd meant it when she told him how sorry she was for his loss. Genuine tears stung her eyes at the funeral because no matter how cantankerous Charlie had been during his lifetime, the fact remained that he'd redeemed himself in the hereafter when he rescued Darci from Terrence's ghost, a fact only she and Charlotte would ever know. Charlie had been laid to rest nearly a week ago, which was the main reason she'd waited so long for this visit.

"I hope this is a social call," Stetson said, looking first at Darci and then the sheriff. "Not official business."

"A little of both, actually." One of Max's rare nervous chuckles echoed off the paneled walls. "I'll let Darci explain."

Damn. She'd sort of hoped Max would use his charm to gloss over the bomb she was about to drop. No such luck. She wiped her palms on her jeans once again before she retrieved the Altoid tin from her purse.

"Well," she said, fidgeting with the raised lettering on the mint container. "I found something that belongs to you. Or at least it does now."

Telling this guy his grandpa was a homicidal maniac who threw an elderly woman to her death down a flight of stairs and lost a family jewel in the process wasn't a revelation she could just

195

blurt out. Okay, part of her was tempted to do just that, veiling her outrage in bluntness. Miss Addie's contempt for Stetson had somehow manifested in Darci, and even though she realized that, it didn't change her opinion of the man. She still couldn't stand him, and probably never would.

"Oh?" Stetson seemed intrigued. "What is it?"

"What it is isn't as important as where it was found."

Max cleared his throat, shot her a subtle look that suggested she weigh her words carefully, just as they'd discussed on the ride across town.

"I'm pretty sure this belonged to your grandfather." Darci opened the little box and very carefully picked up the ruby from inside. She blew on it to get rid of clinging mint dust, then held it out to Stetson. "So that means we found out what happened to the stone he lost from the ring you inherited, the one he had made to celebrate his winning bets on the 1941 Triple Crown winner, Whirlaway."

Stetson's eyes lit up with surprise when he saw the ruby. He held it up to the ring on his finger. The cut and size perfectly matched the three other stones.

"Huh!" A genuine smile appeared on Stetson's face, an expression that suited him much better than the toothy grin that made him look even more like a horse's ass. "Must be my lucky day. Where in the world did you find this? It's been missing for decades."

"That's the interesting part." Darci shifted in

her seat and cracked her knuckles as she searched for the most tactful words to use. "First let me ask you a question. Do you know how your Grandpa Terrence knew Adelaide Brown?"

"Name sounds familiar." Stetson's forehead creased as he thought. Darci was surprised his prissy wife hadn't talked him into getting Botoxed before the election, but that was still a few weeks away. "Who is she?"

"My flower shop used to be her house. We mentioned her when I talked to you about Ellen Morgan and, um, that situation a few months back." Darci shifted in her seat again and waited for him to say something.

"Sorry, I wouldn't have any way of knowing exactly who my grandfather was friendly with." Stetson's gaze slid from Darci to Max, then back again. "Why do you ask?"

"I found this at Petal Pushers, in the cellar. It was under the stairs where the dirt floor met the wall." Darci watched Stetson in case any flicker of guilt flittered across his face to suggest he was aware of the treachery his family committed. "There's only one reason he would've been in Miss Addie's cellar in June of 1941, and I'm afraid it wasn't a pleasant one. Your dad, may God rest his soul, said Terrence lost that stone only days after he got the ring, and pitched a fit about it. It must've made him mad knowing that missing ruby could link him to the scene of Adelaide Brown's murder."

"What?!" Stetson's face contorted as if he'd smelled his own fart. "I'm sorry, but did you just accuse my grandfather of murder? I appreciate you bringing the ruby to me, I really do, but can't you find something more constructive to occupy your time with than barging into my house, *again*, looking for dead bodies?"

"Well, I found one last time, remember?" Darci leaned forward as her sassy mouth reminded him that she'd dug up his Uncle Ellis behind Clydell Manor a few months ago. "Might want to think about that before you get too sanctimonious. Terrence killed Miss Addie in 1941, threw her down the stairs, and made it look like an accident. She died in June, right when he lost that ruby."

"You need to take a look at this." Max took a copy of Miss Addie's letter out of an envelope he'd been holding. He smacked it against his palm a few times before he gave it to Stetson. "We thought you ought to know. And before you two exchange any more heated words, you might want to thank her for not having any inclination to turn this information over to the press."

Stetson jerked the paper from the sheriff's hand. He turned white as he read it. With measured effort, he straightened his features and tried to hide his emotion. Darci couldn't tell whether he was appalled to find out that his grandfather murdered his own brother, and then years later killed a poor old woman to keep her quiet about it, or if Stetson was more worried about losing the election if the paps got a hold of this story.

"This doesn't prove anything. The part about Uncle Ellis is wrong. Daddy said—" Stetson clamped his mouth shut and continued to stare at the document.

Darci figured he was at the part that revealed Terrence as Ellis Clydell's killer, not Titus, and not accidentally, despite what Charlie had said about the matter. Stetson probably thought twice about correcting them on which member of his family murdered the other.

"This letter could've been typed up after she found the ruby." The paper shook in Stetson's hand. He sneered at Darci. "How much do you want to keep quiet about this?"

"Keep your money, but you can kiss my ass!" Rage coursed through Darci. "I returned the ruby, and like Max already told you, I don't have any plans to make this public. You keep talking to me like that, though, and I just might change my mind." Darci took out her new cell phone and pulled up her contacts. "Well, looky here! I've still got Celia Kemp on speed dial."

That shut him up real quick.

"You ought to be ashamed of yourself for talking to her like that." Max wasn't about to let anybody speak to his goddaughter that way. "Come down off that high horse and look at the facts. First off, this letter has been sealed up in a safety deposit bank since two days before Adelaide Brown mysteriously fell to her death at the bottom of those cellar stairs. Secondly, your father told everybody the story about Terrence losing the stone and raising hell about it. If I was a betting man, I'd say that ruby fell out during the struggle. That horse winning the Belmont Stakes, Terrence losing the stone from the ring he had made to celebrate, and Mrs. Brown dying after she confronted him. Kind of a little more than circumstantial, wouldn't you say, since it all happened in 1941, in the span of a week? Unless you have some other big ideas on how to explain why your grandpa, who was running for the same office you're running for now, just happened to lose that stone at the scene of her death?"

Stetson slumped back in his chair, slack-jawed.

"Didn't think so." Max got up to leave. "Come on, Darci."

"Wait." Stetson stared down at the ring on his finger and the ruby that had just turned his world upside down. "Please wait."

Darci thought Stetson was going to vomit. He for damn sure had better not think she was going to hold the garbage can while he heaved into it.

"I'm sorry. I apologize." Holy hell, he looked like he was going to cry. "I shouldn't have spoken to you like that. This is just so hard to process. To think that my grandfather . . . ."

He wasn't able to say the words.

"There's no way you could've known," Max said, being diplomatic.

"Here." Stetson held the ruby out to Darci. "I don't want it. I mean, thank you for returning it, but I can't keep it. Don't want it in this house. You can keep it, sell it, throw it down the sewer for all I care. Just please take it away."

"Thank you." Darci didn't want it either, but she was glad to see Stetson show some sign of humanity.

"No, thank you, for keeping this private."

When Darci frowned and opened her mouth to tell him exactly where he could stick the ruby if he only gave it to her as a bribe to keep her quiet about everything they'd just discussed, Max seemed to read her mind and interrupted.

"See you later, Stetson," he said. Then he put his arm around Darci and led her to the door.

Charlotte was pacing the floor when Darci and Max returned from their trip to Clydell Manor.

"Okay, so that big goofy smile is confusing the hell out of me." Charlotte stopped pacing and stared at her cousin. To Max she said, "Did Stetson knock the rest of the sense clean out of her head?"

"No, but I'll let her tell you herself." Max grinned. "What little sense she had is still rattlin' around in there somewhere." He patted Darci on the back. "See y'all later." He left to go back to his office, a happy spring in his step from the turn of events.

"Oh my God, you're killing me!" Charlotte grabbed Darci's arm and dragged her to the chairs behind the main counter, then pushed her into one. "Tell me what happened or I'm going to choke you."

"It went the total opposite of what we'd expected." Darci leaned back in the chair and put her feet up on the counter beside the computer before she told Charlotte all about her meeting with Stetson. "At least one good thing came out of all this mess." She rattled the jewel heavy Altoid box before she sat it on the desk. "After I figure out where to sell it, that thing should just about cover the deductible for the break in. Might even be enough to buy a small alarm to scare off any other burglars that get ideas about robbing the shop."

The telephone rang.

It was Gene calling Darci with good news. Hattie was going to pull through just fine. She wouldn't have to stay in the hospital much longer, thanks to a new stint in her arteries, and was scheduled to start rehab. When she found out Darci had asked about her, she made her husband call with the news and had him tell her she planned to call herself in the next few days.

Since Darci could not make up her mind about what to tell Hattie, she took the opportunity to ask Gene what he thought was best. He knew Hattie better than anybody, so she would leave the decision up to him. Since Hattie was headed toward a full recovery and her husband was in a wonderful mood, this would be the perfect time to broach the subject.

In light of the recent heart attack, Gene asked Darci not to share the information with Hattie. He thought news of the threat against her grandmother, one that had been made seventy-some years ago, had been a factor is her heart attack. "Probably best to let her believe her Grandma Addie died from the fall. That *is* the truth, so you won't have to feel guilty about holding anything back except the part about somebody helping her along."

She totally agreed with him. Hattie was older

now than Addie had been when she was murdered. Knowing the gruesome truth would only upset her, and it would do nothing to change the way things had played out.

Darci just hoped Miss Addie knew the wrong had been brought to light, the closest they would ever come to giving her justice.

Darci got out of her VW Bug. The car door shut with a hollow thud that made her jump. Sweet Grove Cemetery was deserted except for the cardinals loitering amongst the graves, searching under the leaves for insects to snack on.

She carried two bouquets, each tied with yellow ribbons. Hattie had asked her to put flowers on her grandmother's grave, so Darci ordered fresh daisies, Miss Addie's favorite. When she'd arranged the flowers, she decided to make two bouquets, one from Hattie and other from her own heart.

Darci couldn't explain the odd sensation of putting flowers on Adelaide Brown's grave. Tears filled her eyes as she thanked her for saving her butt not only a couple weeks ago in the cellar, but for all the times she'd swooped in to save the day. It was inexcusable that such a wonderful woman fell victim to the likes of Terrence Clydell while she tried to help Betsy's girls claim their inheritance.

And Terrence had almost gotten away with it,

if not for the stubborn victim refusing to give up even in death.

The strangest part was knowing that only Adelaide Brown's body lay in the grave. Her spirit still lived on at Petal Pushers. Darci didn't know exactly why Miss Addie hadn't crossed to the other side, walked through the pearly gates to join her husband, children, and all the loved ones who had passed on before her. Her unfinished business seemed to have been resolved when her murderer's ruby sparkled in the light in the cellar and found its way into Darci's hands.

Darci put the bouquets in the concrete urns that flanked the tombstone before she turned to walk back down the hill to her car. Her tears had stopped, replaced by a heart full of love for the Ghost Lady, and all the wonderful things she'd brought into Darci's life.

Darci had been afraid that the events in the cellar might have resulted in the spirit crossing over. If ever a soul deserved eternal rest, it was hers. Whatever miracle kept the Ghost Lady at Petal Pushers, Darci was grateful each time she felt a cold spot or heard the unprompted jingle of bells from the closed shop door.

Miss Addie seemed content to stay in her home turned flower shop, tending ailing plants, and watching over the people she cared about.

*Sure am feelin' a whole lot better now that Clydell is gone for good. After all this time, it's*

*good to know things have finally been set straight, what with Clydell's crimes come to light. Sure is a relief not to have to worry about him showing up to hurt Darci, that sweet girl.*

*Thought Hattie was gonna come by for a visit, but maybe before long.*

*I still cain't get over Terrence's boy comin' by to get him out of this house and send him on his way for good. Not sure how things would've turned out if he hadn't. Betsy helped me keep Terrence away from Darci, and there was that other fella that breezed in and pushed Clydell back a couple steps. Not sure who he was, but something about him reminds me of that picture she keeps up front, the one in the silver frame.*

*Oh well, I better go make myself useful. Plenty to be done around here, what with watchin' over Darci, tendin' to the plants and such, keepin' an eye on the little ones when they're upstairs, and entertaining my favorite little bird.*

'This little light of mine, I'm gonna let it shine'. *Hey Daisy, why don't you sing along with me?* 'O-oh this little light of mine, I'm gonna let it shine, let it shine, let it shine.'

# Petal Pushers Plant Profile for
# Shasta Daisy

## *Leucanthemum x superbum*
## Perennial

**Brief description:** The compact bushy plants grow from one to three feet tall. The white flowers with yellow centers are three to five inches wide, and bloom from June through August.

**Trivia:** Daisies symbolize innocence, purity, and new beginnings.

**Growing instructions:** Plant in full sun to partial shade with good drainage, and don't overwater them. Deadhead occasionally to encourage heavier blooms. Cut back the foliage after your daisies finish flowering in late summer.

**Uses:** Daisies are excellent cut flowers, and they are a lovely addition to borders and flower beds.

# Plant and Recipe Index

# Acknowledgements

I want to thank all my family and friends for their love and support, my kids most of all. Amanda, Brittany, Tyler, and Sophie, you're the first to know about my writing projects, give me your honest opinions when I run wild ideas past you, put up with my crazy moods during revisions, and show me those magic moments tucked into each day. Your encouragement means the world to me.

And a big thank you to all my readers.

# About the Author

Photo courtesy of Brittany Hayes

Tina DC Hayes writes romantic suspense and cozy mysteries with a paranormal twist. She lives down a little country road in western Kentucky with her husband and four children. A few pampered pooches and two parrots keep her company while they stand guard against writer's block. In her spare time she reads, hangs out with friends and family, watches movies, plays guitar, and indulges her inner Foodie in the kitchen and by chowing down at cool restaurants. Currently up to her elbows in diapers, she's an expert at 4 a.m. bottle feedings and Patty Cake.

http://tinadchayes.wordpress.com
https://www.facebook.com/TinaDCHayesAuthor
https://twitter.com/Tina_DC_Hayes